"Some changes are more obvious than others."

If merely staring into Mitch's baby blues would cause the sky to fall, Cassie would find out sooner or later. If two years, two thousand miles and at least a million tears hadn't toughened her up, nothing ever would. She might as well find out now.

"Things *have* changed, Mitch," she blurted, finding a surprising strength in her voice as she glared at him. "And despite what your inflated ego might tell you, it'll take a hell of a lot more than a few scrambled eggs, a sexy smile and a slick compliment to make things right again." Crossing her arms protectively over her heart, she took a deep breath and braced for his retort.

He smiled. "Okay," he drawled, nodding agreeably. "I'll buy that. So tell me. What *will* it take, Cassie? What will it take to make you love me again?"

She felt a familiar flutter in her chest and cursed at the way she'd set herself up. "You're impossible," she snapped. "You won't even admit it when you know I'm right."

Their argument was forgotten the moment the window shattered and a bullet hit Samantha, Cassie's mannequin, right between the eyes.

Dear Reader,

Long before I've served the last round of Thanksgiving leftovers, my heart and mind turn with a child's anticipation toward Christmas. Decorating the house comes first. Each room is given a thorough holiday make-over, from the country theme in the dining room to the miniature Santa's toy shop we assemble in the den.

The change in our surroundings seems to trigger a delightful change in our family's routine, as well. Our busy teenagers and our older kids home from college find time to decorate a batch of sugar cookies and help prepare a gift basket for a needy neighbor. My husband and I steal an evening for quiet conversation or meet for lunch in the midst of a hectic shopping day.

After church services on Christmas Eve, steaming bowls of my famous New England clam chowder begin our celebration. As the evening progresses, presents are opened, snapshots taken and somewhere around midnight my husband responds to our clamoring for his own specialty, beef steaks on the grill. Regardless of the weather, our Christmas Eve barbecue has become an indispensable part of our holiday tradition.

On Christmas Day we engage in a variety of games and family foolishness, happily infecting each other with the spirit of the season. And for a few precious hours, the travails of our everyday lives disappear as we reflect upon the precious gift we share—the gift of love.

On behalf of my family, I wish you and the special people in your life the Christmas blessings of peace and love now and throughout the coming year.

Laura Gordon

Scarlet Season

Laura Gordon

Harlequin Books

TORONTO • NEW YORK • LONDON
AMSTERDAM • PARIS • SYDNEY • HAMBURG
STOCKHOLM • ATHENS • TOKYO • MILAN
MADRID • WARSAW • BUDAPEST • AUCKLAND

To the wonderful kids in my life—
Darcy, Heather, Michelle and Todd

ISBN 0-373-22255-6

SCARLET SEASON

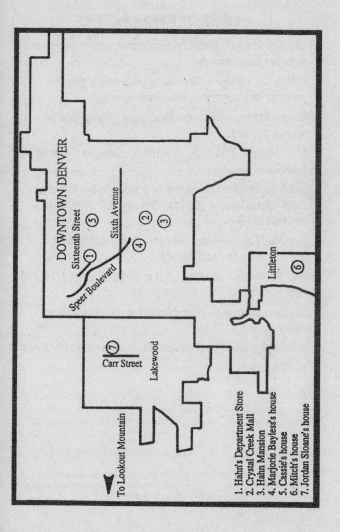

DOWNTOWN DENVER

Sixteenth Street

Sixth Avenue

Speer Boulevard

Littleton

Lakewood

Carr Street

To Lookout Mountain

1. Hahn's Department Store
2. Crystal Creek Mall
3. Hahn Mansion
4. Marjorie Bayless's house
5. Cassie's house
6. Mitch's house
7. Jordan Sloane's house

CAST OF CHARACTERS

Cassie Craig—Her first Christmas home in years was far from merry.

Mitch Dempsey—Time was his enemy when murder stalked the woman he loved.

Grant Hahn—The man had everything, but he wanted more.

Lisa Hahn—The wife of a millionaire, a slave to her passions.

Ruth Palmer—This secretary knew how to take care of the boss—but how far would she go to protect him?

Estelle Hahn—Was everyone's favorite aunt covering up for someone?

Cal Vantana—A man with a secret that cost him his life.

Jordan Sloane—Was this actor playing a dual role?

Arthur Lane—He'd never be a candidate for boss of the year.

Chapter One

He kissed her. The diffused glow coming from the department store windows cast their deep shadows across the glistening pavement. When he lifted his face, she touched his cheek and smiled. And he kissed her again.

Behind the flimsy curtains that ran the length of Hahn's department store windows, Cassie Craig drew a ragged breath and ran a hand through her soft brown shoulder-length curls. A rush of memories—an odd mixture of bitter regret and sweet longing—flooded her.

It happened sometimes, an emotional onslaught triggered by little things. The faint strains of a special song drifting through an open window on a sultry summer night, the sizzling sound of beefsteaks searing on a grill, the distinctive aroma of his cologne while standing in line at the theater. The sight of lovers embracing under a moonless midnight sky.

Despite the sturdy structure of defenses she'd designed to house her battered heart, a chilling draft of pain still managed to seep in sometimes through some small high window left unlatched, or a back door left standing slightly ajar. Even after all this time.

Did it ever happen to him, she wondered, staring a moment at the reflection of her petite frame in the window. That aching longing for the past. That startling pinprick of remembrance and regret.

Cassie gave herself a mental shake, turned her back on the street scene she'd inadvertently witnessed and shoved a box marked Electrical under the ladder at the back of the display. Being downtown again, she told herself, not five blocks from their old apartment, their old stomping grounds, had triggered the memories this time.

"Stop it, Cassie," she ordered, planting one hand on the soft curve of each hip. "You've come too far." Denver to New York and back again. "Too *damn* far to start looking back now." It'd had been two years since she'd last seen Mitch Dempsey. Two years almost to the day. "But who's counting," Cassie muttered, wishing with all her heart she'd stayed home tonight.

A couple of hours ago, as she'd sat in her small kitchen, munching take-out pizza and finalizing the plans for the holiday windows she'd begin in earnest tomorrow, Cassie had realized she needed one last measurement.

Now, standing in the empty store, she focused on her first big project since coming back home and the excitement bubbled up inside her once more. *Everything will work out,* she assured herself as she reached for her jacket, slid into it and dropped the tape measure into her pocket. Her fingers found the wall switch to douse the overhead lights of the large display window. She glanced back out onto the street.

Except for a traffic light at the end of the next block flashing a persistent amber, nothing moved. The lovers had gone. "Good luck," she whispered into the darkness as she turned to leave.

A sudden movement outside the window startled her. A tall, thin man dressed in some sort of dark uniform stood directly in front of the window with his back to the glass. Cassie edged deeper into the window, weeding her way cautiously over boxes and around wiring, not wishing to startle the man she felt sure was unaware of her presence.

A sudden flash of light sent animated shadows dancing through the glass and drew Cassie's attention back out onto the street. The stark glare of high beams split the darkness. The window's interior was illuminated; the entire storefront drenched in white light so glaring Cassie brought her hand up to shield her eyes from the glare.

For one terrifying second, Cassie thought the car might come crashing head-on through the glass. The man outside the window must have had the same thought, because he started running. Suddenly the lights blazed a wide sweep to the right.

The scream that ripped from Cassie's throat when the lights overtook the stumbling man reverberated and amplified against the glass. She felt the sickening thud her mind imagined hearing when the runner was hit, and her stomach lurched. She reached out to steady herself and stumbled backward over the pile of two-by-fours stacked at the back of the display. When she clambered to her feet, there was only darkness. As quickly as the lights had appeared, they'd disappeared.

For one breathless moment Cassie felt welded to the floor, paralyzed by shock and startled disbelief. Chilling dread filled her. Dry mouthed and unblinking, she stared at the motionless figure lying on the sidewalk. When the sudden rush of adrenaline hit her, it was like an electric current jolting her into action.

"Dear God," Cassie whispered as she jumped down out of the display and jogged the obstacle course of hanging displays and long glass counters that crowded the first floor. Past ladies' sportswear and the escalators, she broke into a run, bursting through the hinged doors that led to the employee break room and the store's north side exit.

"Come on, come on," she cried, her hands trembling as she jammed her security card into the electronic lockbox. When she heard the quick buzz disengaging the lock, Cassie slammed her hip against the crash bar in the middle of the heavy metal door and burst out into the alley.

A surge of cold air made her gasp, and an icy rain stung her cheeks like a thousand tiny needles as she raced around the corner of the building toward the figure lying at the edge of the sidewalk where he'd been so brutally struck down.

Choking back the sob that rose in her throat, Cassie dropped down onto her knees beside the still form. His glazed eyes stared unseeing from the chalky depths of his long, pain-twisted face. When he opened his mouth, a thin stream of blood trickled from the corner of his mouth and onto his collar.

Cassie glanced around her, desperately scanning the length of the street. But it was hopeless. She was alone. Alone with a dying man.

Don't move him, some inner voice warned. And then something about shock and keeping the victim warm skittered through her mind.

Oh, please, please, no! a small frightened voice shrieked inside her. *Not me. Not now.* But another voice, a stronger, steadier voice emerged as she shrugged out of her jacket.

"Don't move," she ordered gently, letting that stronger voice take command as she tucked her jacket around his trembling body. "It's all right. Just lie still."

"Help me." His voice was a faint whisper.

"It's all right," she soothed. "I'm going for help. Everything's going to be all right." *Dear God, please let it be true.*

Long, pale fingers reached up and grasped her arm, clutching at the soft yellow sleeve of her sweatshirt as she tried to rise. "Gotta help me," he cried. "K-keys." He choked and sputtered as he tried to sit up, but his efforts proved futile and he fell back gasping in pain. His left leg lay at an odd and unnatural angle beneath him.

"Oh, please," Cassie begged, "please don't try to move. I'll help you," she promised, the cold rain mixed with her own startled tears. "Just lie still."

His shaky hand slid down her arm and groped for her own trembling hand. Finding it, he squeezed with strength born out of desperation. "No," he cried. "Don't leave me. P-please don't go. Must find...must find keys," he whimpered, his voice fading. "P-please, you must help me find . . . them."

The helplessness in his eyes, the desperate sound of his dying voice, so pitiful and pleading, caused a burning lump to swell in Cassie's throat. Her heart bucked against her chest.

"Yes, yes," she promised as she settled his head in her lap, stroked his damp and matted hair, and held his callused hand tighter. "I'll find them," she promised, trying to comfort the stranger with whom she had suddenly become intimate.

"Everything will be all right. We'll find your keys. But I've got to go for help," she explained to him gently as one would reassure a frightened child.

She slid her hand out of the grip that had suddenly lost all strength. His breathing had become shallow and labored; his face and lips had turned a ghastly gray.

"I'll be right back," she promised as she rose. "Right back," she called out again over her shoulder as she raced around the corner.

Cassie ran down the shadowy north side of the building, forcing herself to ignore the ominous darkness of the alleyway. Instead, she focused all of her energies, all of her thoughts on the phone just inside the employee entrance, the call she would make and the help it would bring.

Halfway to the entrance, she heard the sound of tires squealing behind her. She spun around, stumbling, nearly blinded by the blaze of headlights that swept over her, exposing her in their deadly light for one long heart-stopping moment.

The image of the man run down in front of Hahn's sliced through her mind. *You're next!* her horrified mind screamed.

Like a startled deer caught in the middle of the highway and paralyzed by the lights, Cassie stood disbelieving, too stunned to move. But with her next heartbeat, reality broke through and the instinct for survival took over.

As the car bore down on her, she raced for the doorway without looking back. She still clutched the plastic security card in her hand; the awful knowledge that she'd never have time to use it mocked her. Even if she could make it to the entrance, the shallow doorway would offer little protection. In the next moment, her pursuer would overtake her and she would be run down or crushed mercilessly against the cold brick building.

Just as her desperate thoughts threatened to consume her, Cassie's eyes locked on the two huge metal dumpsters beside the employee entrance. Without another thought, she dove behind them. Concrete and gravel bit into her hands and her screams slit the night air as the car roared past her.

A moment later, still huddled behind her hulking protectors, Cassie heard tires squeal again as the car swerved out onto the street at the other end of the alley. The sound of the engine faded away into the night.

Alone once more in the darkness, Cassie began to shake almost uncontrollably as the shock and reality of what had just happened crashed down around her.

Staggering to her feet, she hurried to the door. How she steadied her hand to whisk the security card through the slot at the bottom of the lockbox she'd never know.

A few seconds later, inside the deserted store, Cassie clutched the phone to her ear and dialed 911. "Please, oh, please!" she cried, when she heard the blessed sound of an anonymous voice on the other end of the line. "Please, somebody help me!"

SHE HEARD THE high-pitched wail of sirens almost before she hung up the phone. The fact that help was on the way should have reassured her, but the eerie sound sent a new series of anxious shivers skittering down Cassie's spine.

At the exit, she ran her security card through the slot on the lockbox and waited for the sound of the electronic click. When she didn't hear the lock disengage, she tried pushing against the crash bar anyway, but it wouldn't budge. Cassie passed the small plastic card through the slot again, but still the door remained firmly locked.

"Come on," she breathed impatiently. Maybe the card had gotten wet or bent, she thought, and swiped the magnetic strip across her sleeve. This time she inserted the card into the machine with authority. Nothing.

"Damn it," she shouted, and jammed the card back into the slot over and over again. When the lock finally disengaged with a faint click, Cassie hit the crash bar full force. The door flew open and she grabbed for the metal bar to keep from falling face first out onto the alley. Regaining her balance quickly, Cassie ran around to the front of the building.

The quiet street had been transformed into a bustling scene, bursting with sound and motion. Flashing lights curled up and around the long canyon of towering glass-and-steel buildings, sending glowing streamers of red shimmering skyward. Faceless voices coming from police and emergency dispatchers crackled with discord and echoed eerily through the night.

Cassie hurried over to the ambulance at the same time the attendants pulled the double doors at the back of the vehicle closed.

"How is he?" she asked breathlessly.

A tall, blond, uniformed policeman moved up beside her. "Are you the one who called in the hit and run?"

Cassie nodded. "Yes, yes, I am. How is he? Is he going to be all right?" Something was wrong. Cassie knew it by the way the cop's dark eyes studied her.

"Ma'am, can you tell me exactly where the accident took place?"

"Why, here! Right here." Cassie pointed to the spot on the pavement where the stranger had lain.

"Are you sure, ma'am?"

"Of course, I'm sure," Cassie said without hesitation.

The policeman stared at her a moment longer before asking, "And just when did this supposed hit and run take place?"

Supposed? What did that mean? "Why, just a few minutes ago..." Cassie glanced down at her watch, it was a little past midnight. "Not over five or ten minutes, I guess. I ran out onto the street the moment it happened. I suppose I should have called you first, but..."

Cassie felt the ambulance attendants staring at her. "But it all happened so fast. I was in the window—the display window. I work there," she explained, pointing to Hahn's. "I was leaving for the night, when I saw him outside the window. Just standing there, alone. Like he was waiting for someone, maybe. Anyway, as I turned to leave, a car with the brightest lights—high beams, I guess, came roaring down the street. I was afraid the car was coming through the window. And then he started to run..."

"The man standing outside the window?" the officer asked.

Cassie nodded, glancing over her shoulder at the ambulance. "Yes. He tried to get away, but the lights...they kept coming." Cassie looked over her shoulder again. Why was everyone just standing and staring? Why weren't they working over the injured man in the back of the ambulance?

"What's going on?" Cassie blurted, casting an accusing glare first at the policeman and then at the idle ambulance crew. "Why aren't you on your way to the hospital?" she demanded. But even as she asked the question, the terrible answer crept into her consciousness.

Her hands flew up to her mouth as the awful truth broke through. It was too late. There was no longer any need to hurry, no need for expediency or desperate lifesaving measures. He'd died. She hadn't reached help in time. A devastating sense of loss and dreadful emptiness lodged heavily in the pit of her stomach as a picture of the man whose hand she'd held, whose fears she'd tried to allay took shape in her mind.

"He's dead, isn't he?" she asked in a voice barely audible.

"No, ma'am," the officer reassured, touching her elbow and coaxing her toward the police cruiser parked at the curb. "No one has died. Now if you'll just come with me, I'd like to ask you a few more questions."

"Wh-what? What's going on here?" Cassie demanded to know, shaking free of his touch.

"Ma'am, that's exactly what I'm trying to find out. Now, if you'll just come with me." This time the grip on her arm was stronger, less polite and definitely more official.

VISIONS OF A LONG, relaxing shower, a tall, cold Coors and eight hours of gloriously uninterrupted sleep disintegrated before Mitch Dempsey's blue eyes as the dispatcher's words "hit and run" and "window dresser" landed in his solar plexus with the force of a physical blow.

Wrenching the steering wheel of his '67 Porsche 911 hard to the left, Mitch stomped down on the accelerator and slashed across three lanes of deserted boulevard. Rubber fought for traction on the glazed pavement, and the rear tires bounced against the curb before fishtailing back into the street.

Grabbing the car phone, Mitch punched up the number and barked out the question that was burning a hole through his brain.

"The Hahn's employee was only a witness," the dispatcher quickly assured him. "She wasn't involved in the accident or hurt in any way, as far as we can tell."

Mitch took a sharp left without signaling. "Did you get her name, Tommy?"

"Mitch? What's up? You sound kinda . . . weird."

The dull ache between his eyes was beginning to throb. "Just give me her name, Tommy," Mitch demanded. "What was the window dresser's name?"

"Cassandra Craig. Hey, what's going on, Mitch?" the voice on the other end wanted to know. "I thought you'd gone home."

"Yeah, well . . . I'm back."

Chapter Two

"But you've got to listen!" Cassie pleaded with the uniformed officer who had flipped his notebook closed. "You must belive me. He was here! Right here," she insisted, pointing to the exact spot where, not more than ten minutes ago, she'd held a dying man's hand and promised to help.

"Well, he's not here now, is he?" the patrolman countered. His steady stare rested on Cassie, unblinking. "And there was no one here when the ambulance arrived."

As the officer walked around to the driver's side of his black-and-white cruiser, Cassie was on his heels.

"You have to do something," she insisted, her voice rising. "There's a man out there somewhere—badly hurt. Maybe even dying! Someone deliberately ran him down and then tried to do the same thing to me!"

The policeman released an impatient sigh. "Okay, ma'am, if this guy was in as bad a shape as you say he was, how'd he just up and leave?"

"How should I know?" Cassie snapped, frustration and anger vying for possession of her emotions. All at once, a hopeful possibility dawned.

"Maybe someone else came by. That could have happened, couldn't it?" She searched the officer's face for some sign of agreement. "While I was running for my life in the alley or inside calling for help, maybe someone drove by, saw the injured man and took him to the hospital."

The policeman shook his head. "I doubt it. When someone in that condition is taken to an emergency room, the police are notified. It's been a quiet night. If he had been taken to a hospital, we'd have heard. I'm sure by now every cop in town has heard about your hit and run."

"It's not *my* hit-and-run," Cassie said. "It's not my *anything!*" Resentment welled inside. Somewhere along the way she'd been placed on the defensive and she didn't like the feeling one bit. "That poor man was lying over there on the sidewalk...right over there!"

Cassie's nerves, stretched tighter than piano wire, vibrated with renewed shock. The chilling rain had subsided, but it had taken its toll as well. Her clothes were damp and the sharp breeze that had risen in the past few moments drove a bone-numbing chill to the center of her being.

"Listen," the officer said gently, coming up beside her and resting his hand on her shoulder. "Maybe the guy just passed out, you know? These street guys— hard-core winos, mostly, sometimes they look as though they're on their last legs, you know what I mean?"

Cassie shrugged away from his touch, her back stiffening with angry indignation. "I know what I saw, Officer. A man was run down." She swallowed the catch in her voice before continuing. "Do you understand? He was not a wino...or a drunk. I saw the whole thing. I talked to the man." I touched him, Cassie thought. And in some inexplicable way, she realized the stranger had touched her, as well.

"And I can tell you, it was no wino behind the wheel of that car in the alley that tried to run me down!" she insisted.

The policeman, his official demeanor firmly back in place, was clearly unconvinced. "I'm sorry, ma'am, but there's just nothing to back up your story. No victim. No car. Not even a skid mark. You can't even give us a description of the vehicle."

No, she couldn't give him the concrete information that would make her story believable, she admitted. "The lights against the glass produced a blinding glare," she explained, as much for his information as for her own peace of mind. And of course there wouldn't have been any skid marks, the car hadn't tried to stop. The attack against the stranger outside of Hahn's and against her in the alleyway had been deliberate, Cassie realized with sudden and stark objectivity.

The officer pressed his card into her hand. "If you remember anything else that might help us get a fix on what you claim happened here tonight—"

"I didn't imagine any of this," Cassie interrupted. "I've told you exactly what happened here tonight."

"Cassie?"

The sound of the deep baritone behind her scattered her thoughts like buckshot. The familiar resonance reached out with an invisible force and turned her around to face a pair of unforgettable blue eyes. One look, and the torrent of memories left her breathless.

Mitch. Without a sound, his name formed on her lips and, like Alice through the looking glass, Cassie wondered for one crazy moment if the whole bizarre evening had been a dream.

"Detective Dempsey," the uniformed officer addressed Mitch, "I've already taken Ms. Craig's statement. Would you like to take a look?"

Mitch acknowledged the patrolman with a vague nod, ignoring the notebook the officer held out to him. Mitch's deep blue-eyed gaze—long, lingering, devouring—fastened firmly on Cassie's own startled green eyes and held her mesmerized.

When he finally shifted his attention to the uniformed officer, Cassie released her long-held breath. Her lungs burned as she fought the feeling of lightheadedness that made her knees weak and tugged her body toward the pavement. Closing her eyes, she inhaled a deep, cleansing, steadying breath, trying to will her reeling emotions still.

"So what do we have here, Sommerfield?" Mitch asked.

Cassie opened her eyes and clasped her arms around herself as she listened critically to Officer Sommerfield's curt summation of the "alleged hit and run," adding his own theory of how the lights shining through the display had more than likely distorted Cassie's perceptions of the events taking place outside of the glass.

She pinned him with an icy glare; if looks could indeed render bodily harm, the ambulance crew would have had their hands full tending to the wounded officer.

As Sommerfield went on to explain how he'd arrived on the scene to find nothing but a string of emergency vehicles and a distraught witness, Cassie was forced to consider for the first time just how incredible her story sounded.

"Cover every inch of this sidewalk and search the alley," Mitch ordered as another police car pulled up to the curb. "The two of you divide the area," he said, nodding to the second patrolman as he emerged from his cruiser. "I'll take a final statement from Ms. Craig and check in with you tomorrow."

Mitch dismissed Sommerfield and the second officer with an official tone Cassie couldn't recall ever hearing him use before. As she watched the two men sweep the area with their flashlights, Cassie shivered. Mitch shrugged out of his jacket and draped it over her shoulders. Instinctively she snuggled into it and discovered Mitch's distinctive scent and his personal warmth still clinging to every fiber. Without thinking, she inhaled, savoring the familiar essence.

When he put his arm around her, Cassie didn't resist, but moved mechanically toward his car parked at the curb.

Mitch would at least listen, she told herself. He'd know how to help her. He'd know what to do.

A silent snow had started to fall, and huge lacy crystals formed a white coating over the shimmering pavement. As the ambulance and emergency vehicles pulled away and turned at the corner, disappearing from view, the street fell into a muted semidarkness; the only sound was the distant rumble of a city bus groaning to a stop some blocks away.

When Mitch opened the car door, Cassie climbed in, wondering if, somewhere in this cold, lonely city the stranger had found help.

Mitch gunned the engine to life and blessed heat poured out from the vents on the floor, warming Cassie's numbed feet and ankles. After a moment, he said softly, "It's good to see you again, Cass."

The unexpected tenderness in his voice, the ease with which the old endearment had slid from his lips caused a tiny flutter in her chest.

"So just what *did* happen here tonight?"

Cassie released a long breath and shook her head. "Thinking back, the whole thing almost seems unreal." With her emotions unsettled, could she trust her voice to say more?

She felt him studying her face. "Can you remember anything about the car? Was the car that came after you in the alleyway the same car that ran the man down?"

Cassie shook her head again. "I don't know. The glare from the headlights in the alleyway was blinding."

"Do you think you would recognize the victim again if you saw him?"

She nodded. "Of course." Cassie saw the stranger's ashen face staring out at her from her memory.

"Did he say anything, do anything that might help us identify him?"

"He never told me his name." Would she ever forget the terrified look in the stranger's eyes or the sound of his voice, pleading and pitifully choked with pain? "I wasn't sure what to do for him. I was so afraid... he'd die."

Mitch studied her with an expression of intense concern. Cassie averted her gaze from that patented Dempsey look. It made her heart race and her hands go clammy, but she must never again mistake it for love, she warned herself.

When she glanced up, she saw Sommerfield moving toward the Porsche. Mitch got out of the car and walked with him over to the other policeman standing beside his cruiser. The three men exchanged a few words before Sommerfield turned away and the two cruisers pulled out into the street together.

As Cassie watched Mitch walking back to the Porsche, she was struck again by his official bearing. No way around it, Mitch Dempsey was still one of the best looking men she'd ever seen. He wore his wavy black hair much longer than he had a couple of years ago. No doubt, leaving the patrolman's uniform behind for the detective's badge had given him the personal freedom to make the change. It was a change Cassie admitted that she liked.

But aside from his hair, little else had changed. Tonight, Mitch Dempsey was every inch the professional she remembered, one trained to deal with hysterical victims and shell-shocked witnesses. He'd always possessed a rare mixture of toughness and compassion, gentleness and strength, characteristics that made him a natural for his profession.

And he was only doing his job now, Cassie reminded herself firmly, just as Sommerfield and the ambulance attendants had done theirs. Her inner voice warned that this feeling of intimacy that had wrapped itself around her senses like a warm blanket was only a false perception brought on by the stress of the situation and her own confused emotions.

"Did they find anything?" she asked when he slid behind the steering wheel and closed the door.

Mitch shook his head. "Don't be discouraged, Cass. Later you could remember something about the car," he assured her, draping his arm casually across the back of the seat. "Sometimes it takes a few days or even weeks and then out of the blue, a witness remembers everything, right down to the last detail."

Cassie nodded but felt unconvinced.

"We'll keep at it," he said, and slid his arm down onto her shoulders. His hand pressed reassuringly against her arm.

We? And just who does that 'we' include? Cassie wondered. Mitch, the cop? Or Mitch, the man, the ex-fiancé? The Mitch, who after just one look, she knew she'd have to start trying to forget all over again? Cassie's heart lurched against her chest and then sank as a feeling of renewed loss washed over her. She'd lost more than her lover two years ago; she'd lost her best friend, as well.

"You know, I've been thinking about what Sommerfield said about the glare coming through the windows," Mitch began. "It could have given you a distorted image of what really happened outside the display."

Like a splash of icy creek water, the vulnerability of her position slapped her. She felt as if she were falling, the events of the long evening spinning her wildly out of control. And from where she sat—here in the dark with Mitch Dempsey's arm tucked firmly around her—she could almost feel the pain of another crash landing.

In one fluid motion, she was out of the car and striding across the sidewalk. When she felt his hand on her arm, she spun around to face him, the angry tears that welled in her eyes made him a sparkling presence before her.

"Damn you," she cried jerking away from his touch. "Something happened here tonight! Something terrible, and whether or not the Denver Police Department or you, Detective Dempsey, choose to believe it, I know what I saw!"

She nearly stumbled when she whirled around and marched blindly toward the red mountain bike she'd left chained up near the employee entrance.

"Cassie!" he called after her.

She hesitated only an instant, cursing how the mere sound of his voice uttering her name weakened her resolve.

"Cassie, wait. I want to help."

"Forget it," she shouted without looking back. *I can't go the distance with you, Dempsey. You don't fight fair.* "Sommerfield has my statement. He can call me if he needs anything else."

"But, Cassie," he called out again, "I believe you."

She stopped walking, but she didn't turn around when she felt him move up beside her. "You heard Sommerfield. There's no body. No skid marks. Nothing. No one to back up my claim. As far as the police are concerned nothing happened," she said bitterly.

"But something did happen and you saw it." It wasn't a question, but a pure statement of fact. He placed both hands gently on her shoulders and turned her around to face him.

She stood staring at him, desperate to regain some sort of mental equilibrium. If he really did believe her, then for the first time in the whole long, miserable evening, she would feel less alone. Looking into those very blue eyes, common sense screamed for her to duck and run. Whether he believed her or not, getting involved with Mitch Dempsey again wasn't merely stupid, it was emotional suicide.

"Of all the cops in this city," she groaned, "it had to be you."

She could have predicted the self-satisfied smile that stole across his handsome face. It was one of a dozen little things about him she'd always found irresistibly charming. And so, despite his smile, or maybe because of it, the decision was made. She'd trust him.

"Talk to me, Cassie," he prodded, his voice soft and disarming, not an ounce of professionalism showing.

"I'll never forget that poor man," Cassie began. "He was terribly hurt, Mitch. He was going to die." She cleared the catch in her voice and went on, her words tumbling over each other. "He kept talking about his keys. Can you imagine that? His body all twisted and broken and he begged me to help him find his keys." She took a shaky breath.

Mitch's face betrayed nothing as he reached into the side pocket of his leather jacket and pulled out a small dark object. Taking her hand, he turned it over and dropped a cloth bag into her open palm.

Cassie grasped the wet parcel that felt strangely heavy for its size and moved closer to the window where the security lights from inside Hahn's would allow her to examine it more closely.

The bag was velvet and, though sodden and black, Cassie guessed it might have originally been a deep red or purple jeweler's bag. It was closed at the top with a tiny drawstring.

"My money says there's a set of keys inside," Mitch said.

Quickly Cassie pulled the bag open and drew out the contents. As Mitch had predicted, it was a set of keys attached to a thin gold ring.

"Where did you get these?" she demanded. "And why didn't you show them to Sommerfield?" she asked accusingly. "He might have believed me if you had."

"I found the bag in the gutter when I pulled up at the curb. And it was exactly because Sommerfield didn't believe you that I kept my discovery to myself."

"But why?"

"Cops are only human, Cass. I wanted to give you a chance to take a look at these before I turned them over to a man who'd be all too eager to explain them away—along with your story, just to save face."

Cassie nodded, admitting to herself that he might be right about Sommerfield. Mitch's innate sense of human nature, she remembered, had always been keen.

Returning her attention to the keys, she realized it didn't really matter why Mitch had withheld the evidence he'd found. What mattered was that by doing so, he'd given her the chance to examine the keys that meant more to a dying man than his own life.

Together they stared at Mitch's find as Cassie turned the keys over in her hand again. Somehow, it wasn't the three keys, nor the ring holding them that most captured Cassie's attention, but rather the heavy metal object dangling from the ring. Cassie held the small shining replica of an automobile closer to the light.

"Do you think it's real?" she asked.

"Gold?"

She nodded and handed him the key ring.

Mitch examined the charm more closely. "It could be. It's certainly heavy enough to be real. Maybe the value of this little trinket had something to do with our man's strange preoccupation with finding it."

"Whatever the reason, he was desperate to find these," Cassie said sadly. "If only I could reassure him somehow, let him know I'd found them. Do you think these keys are enough to convince the police to open an official investigation?"

Mitch smiled as he dropped the keys back into their pouch and drew the string closed. "It doesn't matter," he said softly. "It's enough for me."

"I CAN'T BELIEVE you tried to convince me to let you ride this thing home," Mitch said as he rolled Cassie's bike down the hallway.

"Here it is," she said when he started to roll her bike past her door. "I live in 302."

"But downstairs in the lobby your name is on the mailbox marked 304."

"Always the cop," she murmured. "It's a mix-up with the mailbox keys," she explained. "The guys who lived in my apartment before I did never turned their keys in to the super. Three-O-four is vacant, so I'm using that mailbox until a new key can be made."

Cassie was acutely aware of his presence as he shook the snow from his thick dark hair and waited for her to open the door. She still felt shaken by the experiences of the past hour, and despite her need to believe otherwise, she was glad he was with her.

"Well, thanks for the ride," she said after finally locating her keys, slipping them into the lock and pushing the door open. Taking hold of the handlebars, she eased the bike from his grip. "I guess now that I'm back in the land of sudden storms I'll be driving my car more often."

"Where's your brandy?" Mitch asked moving past her across the small living room and into the galley kitchen.

"Mitch..." Cassie protested from the door as she stepped out of her shoes and shrugged off his jacket. "It's late," she said, coming up behind him.

But he'd already found the brandy and glasses, and he handed her a half-filled snifter as he walked past her toward the life-size, elegantly dressed mannequin standing in front of the glass doors in the dining area.

"Still hanging around with the same rough crowd, I see," he quipped, patting the mannequin's slim posterior. "It's been a long time, Samantha," he said with a wry grin. "How's it going?"

Cassie smiled in spite of herself. "I don't think she remembers you. As you said, it has been a long time."

"Oh, I wouldn't be so sure of that," Mitch said, his intense stare issuing the challenge. "Something tells me that behind that cool Mona Lisa smile lies a warm heart."

"Behind that cool smile, Detective Dempsey," Cassie shot back, "lies an even cooler head. But you may be right. Some things are difficult to forget."

Cassie broke the staring war they'd unofficially declared and walked into the living room, dropping down onto the overstuffed love seat and curling her still-frozen feet up under her. Mitch followed her, moving across the room with the same athletic grace she'd always admired.

Instinctively Cassie stiffened when he sat down beside her. Over the rim of her snifter, she studied his suddenly serious expression and realized she'd made a big mistake. Her flip comment had opened a personal door through which they'd both stepped much too easily.

"It's been a long night," she said softly.

He nodded. "It has." He set his glass down quickly and rose to his feet.

An unwelcome sense of loss began to well inside her as he picked up his jacket and headed for the door.

"Breakfast still your favorite meal of the day?" he asked, one hand on the doorknob. His quick return to a light, conversational tone caught her off guard.

"Yes, but—"

"Good. I still hate it and you probably still don't know how to cook it. Pick you up at ten and we'll call it brunch."

Cassie got to her feet. "Mitch, I don't know if that's such a good idea...."

He seemed not to have heard. "I don't think there's anything more we can hope to accomplish tonight. See you in the morning, Cass."

Further protest died on her lips as he pulled the door closed behind him. Her hand was on the knob when he pushed the door back open.

"Why don't you keep these," he suggested, dropping the small velvet bag into her hand. "Bring them with you tomorrow and we'll try to figure out what to do with them."

His fingertip grazed her cheek when he brushed back a damp curl that had fallen there. His brows drew together in a dark, speculative frown as he studied her face for another long moment. "Do you think he saw you, Cassie?"

"Of course he saw me," she answered. "I told you he spoke to me, told me about the keys..."

"No, Cassie. Not the victim," he explained in a low voice. "The driver. Do you think the driver saw you?"

The implication behind his words sent fear slithering through her, coiling itself around her senses like a deadly reptile.

"I—I don't know. I had already turned off the overhead lamps in the display, but the security lights inside the store were on, of course. The light from his high-beams lit up the whole window...and then, in the alley...yes—yes, he must have seen me then," she said, bringing her hands up to her temples, which had suddenly begun to throb.

His silent scrutiny was maddening.

"What are you thinking?" she urged him. "Tell me, Mitch. What is it?"

He ran a hand through his hair and sighed. "I don't know, Cass. I'm probably just being paranoid. But we can't afford to take any chances...with a situation that's so uncertain."

"Come on, Dempsey. Save the cop mumbo jumbo. What are you trying to say?" Cassie demanded, alarm tightening like a twisted rubber band in her stomach.

"I'm sorry, Cass," he said, his expression softening. "I didn't mean to frighten you, but I can't seem to stop the cop in me from worrying. Humor me, okay? Double check the locks before you go to bed tonight."

He reached into his pocket, pulled out a small white card and pressed it into her hand. "My home number is on there. Call me if you need anything. Anything," he repeated, his expression taut again. "Now get some sleep. I'll see you in the morning."

When he'd gone, Cassie closed the door and leaned against it for a full moment, letting the stark realities of the night sink in. She'd witnessed a brutal and deliberate hit and run, her own life had been narrowly preserved, and now, unbelievably, Mitch Dempsey was back in her life.

She glanced down at the card in her hand and quickly committed to memory the handwritten numbers scrawled on the back. What kind of fool was she, anyway? How could she even consider calling on the man who'd broken every promise he'd ever made to her?

The answer that came back to her was the only one she could accept—at least for now—and that answer had to do with Mitch, the cop. If she ever hoped to discover the truth of what had happened tonight, she'd need some help, the kind of help that Mitch with his official connections could provide.

She shoved the card into her pocket and double-checked the locks on the front door and the double glass doors that faced the street, before heading for the bedroom.

The sound of the telephone's shrill ring startled her. Could Mitch be home already? she wondered as she grabbed for the phone next to her bed.

"Hello?"

"Ms. Craig? Cassandra Craig?"

"Yes," Cassie answered. She didn't recognize the voice. Alarm prickled up her spine; who could be calling at this hour and why?

"Ms. Craig, this is Scott Avery. I'm a reporter from the *Herald.* I got your name from Denver PD—from an Officer Sommerfield. I have your case number if you need more verification."

Cassie said she did, and Avery repeated the number that Sommerfield had jotted down on the card he'd given her.

"Ms. Craig, would you mind if I ask you a few quick questions about what happened tonight outside of Hahn's?"

Cassie felt a wave of apprehension rippling though her. "Why, I don't know," she hesitated, trying to gather her thoughts. "It's late...."

"This will only take a few minutes. I don't know if your story is something we'll decide to use, but we like to follow up on the calls that come in. You must admit, Ms. Craig, your story is unusual."

"Yes, I guess it is...."

"The police said there were no other witnesses."

"That's right," Cassie said, remembering with a shudder how truly alone she'd felt. If only there had been another witness, what a difference it would have made in the outcome of this harrowing evening.

"Ms. Craig?" the reporter broke into her speculations. "Are you still there?"

Cassie made her decision. Maybe someone else *had* seen something tonight in front of Hahn's. And perhaps reading the newspaper article would prompt that someone to come forward and corroborate her story.

"I had just finished working when it happened ..." she began.

Scott Avery's questions were brief and succinct, but relating the events of the hit and run and the subsequent attack in the alley seemed to drain every ounce of Cassie's energy.

When she told him she'd found something at the scene that she believed belonged to the victim, Avery pressed her to tell him what it was.

"It's nothing of real value," she explained cautiously. "If he reads the article, he'll know." If by some miracle the hit-and-run victim was still alive, he could contact the newspaper, Cassie reasoned, and they, in turn, could contact her.

Surprisingly, Scott Avery seemed to agree. "You're probably right. If we say too much about it, we'll be deluged with calls from people trying to lay their claim."

Five minutes later, Cassie hung up the phone, feeling edgy and exhausted. Her conversation with the reporter swirled around in her mind, and a vague uneasiness settled over her like a heavy woolen blanket. Her neck and shoulders screamed with accumulated tension and her palms still stung from the dive she'd taken in the alley.

Sleep, Mitch had said. *Ha! Easy for him to say,* Cassie thought as she prepared for bed. Her churning thoughts kicked up a torrent of unrest that made the prospect of sleep an impossibility.

Picking up the small velvet pouch that lay on the nightstand, Cassie took out the keys and examined them again, more closely. Three keys, just ordinary keys. The small replica of an automobile wasn't over two inches in length and remarkable only in its detail, from the small winged figure perched on the hood to the graceful curve of its wide fenders.

But even if its tiny wheels and stylized chassis were cast of pure gold, how much could it be worth, Cassie wondered. What value did the little charm possess that could possibly make it more important than a life?

Chapter Three

The waiting had been torturous and now—damn it—he was down to his last two cigarettes. He'd have to go back out sooner or later, but not before the call.

When the phone finally rang, he jumped. Its second shrill demand was cut short as the smoker grabbed the receiver from its cradle and pressed it to his ear. A salutation was unnecessary; the call had been prearranged, expected.

"Is it over?" the caller's cultured voice asked simply.

"Yes" came the quick reply; their conversation couldn't be concluded fast enough as far as he was concerned.

"Then the terms of our agreement have been fulfilled?"

Another stub was ground out into an overflowing ashtray near the phone. "There was a slight problem. It wasn't on him." A fine sheen of cold sweat rose on his forehead.

"Find it, you fool!" The command was a taut bark that welcomed no explanations or arguments.

He lit his last cigarette. The small, dark bedroom was momentarily illuminated by the flickering blue blaze. Even to his tainted senses, the air smelled stale and sour.

"I can't go back there," he began. "There could have been a witness. The police were called."

The gasp was a choking sound. "Stupid fool!" The indictment was a deadly hiss, followed by a prickly moment of silence that promised menace as surely as any spoken threat. "I don't pay for jobs half-finished. But believe me, *you* will pay if you don't deliver."

"But what about the witness?" The smoker kneaded the burning cords at the base of his neck with one clammy palm.

"I want those keys," the caller hissed, "and with or without you I mean to get them. If there's a problem with a witness, you know what must be done."

For some moments after the caller hung up, the man sat in darkness, sorting out his limited options. First and foremost, he had to get his hands on that money. He'd worked too hard, taken too many risks to walk away now. Besides, what future did he have without the money?

He'd have to find those damned keys or prove they didn't exist. Afterward, he'd tie up the loose ends—the witness. There was no question of what had to be done. One way or another, the witness had to be silenced. Just what she'd seen, he didn't know. But the stakes were too high to take chances. Life or death. His or hers. The decision was easy; the witness would have to die so that he could live.

"I DON'T UNDERSTAND how you could have done something so damn foolish."

Cassie bristled under Mitch's accusation and answered him with a look of glaring indignation. Maybe keeping this relationship all business would be easier than she'd thought.

"Sorry you don't approve," she snapped, lowering the fork poised above a plate crowded with a steaming Denver omelet, a generous portion of hash browns and two poppy-seed muffins. All she needed now was an appetite, something Mitch Dempsey's latest remarks had effectively and completely killed.

"I saw nothing wrong with telling my story to Scott Avery last night." Cassie only wished she felt as confident as she sounded.

Silence stretched itself tightly between them until the waitress who brought Cassie's orange juice moved away from the booth. Cassie could feel Mitch staring at her as she poked at her omelet.

"Setting yourself up as a target for every kook and weirdo who can read was very naive, Cassie."

Cassie's cheeks burned and her pulse pounded angrily in her throat. Though, at twenty-seven, she was five years younger than Mitch and admittedly less accustomed to the darker side of human nature he was exposed to almost daily, it'd been a long time since anyone had accused her of being naive. She dropped the fork and grabbed her purse.

"I knew this was a rotten idea," she muttered over her shoulder as she grabbed the check and headed for the door.

His hand caught hers as she brushed past him.

"Cassie, sit down."

She glared at him and then down at his hand still holding hers. Immediately he released her.

"Please?" he added softly. When Cassie didn't move, he said, "Okay, okay, I may have overreacted. I'm sorry. Now will you please sit down. We've got a lot of ground to cover before the trail gets too cold to follow."

Encouraged by his reference to their joint, albeit unofficial, investigation, Cassie relented and slid back into the booth.

"Look, I honestly don't see what possible harm the article can do, Mitch," she said.

He shook his head, his expression somber. "That's just the problem, we don't know what kind of response it might trigger."

"But I told you Avery guaranteed my anonymity," she reminded him.

Mitch looked unimpressed. Cassie stared down at her food. The clattering sounds coming from the restaurant's small kitchen and conversation from the other diners seated around them filled their uneasy silence. After a moment, he reached across the table and covered her hand with his. She looked up at him, trying to ignore the electric effect of his touch.

"Sorry," he said softly, "but I don't much like it that someone tried to use you as a target last night in that alley."

"And I do?" Cassie suppressed a shudder. "But if someone is out there who saw or heard something that I missed last night, we need to know about it, don't we?"

Mitch nodded his tentative agreement, his expression still grim.

"Avery said the article would be short. After all," she added with a sardonic smile, "the *Herald* isn't likely to give much coverage to an event that, according to the police, never happened."

The frown lines across Mitch's forehead deepened. "I checked with dispatch this morning. There were no reports of anyone matching the description you gave checking in to Denver General emergency last night, no vehicle-pedestrian accident victims, either." He went on to relate the details of the conversation he'd had earlier that morning with his chief. Neither Cassie's story nor the set of keys they'd found in the street were enough to trigger an official investigation.

"Well, then the article might not be such a bad place to start," Cassie said, not really expecting him to agree.

"I've taken some time off," Mitch put in casually.

"A vacation?"

"Sort of," he admitted. "But I won't be going anywhere. I'll be in town." He didn't look at her as he spoke, but focused intently on the contents of his coffee cup instead.

"How did you ever manage to get time off so easily?" she asked, remembering the old days when an unscheduled day off from the force was nearly impossible to secure.

"Oh, I'd already scheduled it some time ago," he countered quickly.

Instinctively Cassie knew he was hedging and couldn't help wondering why.

"And since I'll have the time," he went on, "I'll do some poking around to see what I can come up with. First, I plan to take our mysterious keys to a locksmith. If we can find out what kind of locks they fit, it might help us get a line on their owner."

Cassie pulled the small velvet bag out of her purse and handed it to him. All of the sudden she knew beyond a doubt that Mitch had taken time off work for the sole purpose of launching his own investigation into the hit and run.

A feeling of gratitude welled up inside her, but in the next moment that feeling was replaced by a stab of apprehension. This wasn't going to be easy. The Mitch she remembered, the Mitch she'd fallen in love with three years ago would have done the same thing.

"Well, I'm not on vacation," she announced, her voice sounding tight. "And I'd better get over to Hahn's. The wooden soldiers I've ordered should be coming in this afternoon. If I hear anything," Cassie said as she swallowed her first and last bite of the omelet and stuffed a poppy-seed muffin into her purse for later, "I'll call you."

Mitch tossed a ten onto the table and followed her out of the restaurant. "If you hear anything?"

"If there is a reaction to the newspaper article, I asked Scott Avery to call me."

"Do you trust this guy, Cass?" he asked as they stepped out into the midmorning sunlight and crisp Colorado air.

"Why shouldn't I?" she countered as they walked toward her car. "Listen, I know you cops are sensitive when it comes to the media, but not every reporter is looking for a story to exploit. I don't think Avery had any ulterior motives.''

He shook his head and smiled a grim smile of resignation. ''Cassandra Craig, you're hopelessly trusting.''

She knew it was the truth. And hopeful and trusting were the very things she couldn't afford to allow herself to feel around Mitch Dempsey.

''Please don't lecture me,'' she blurted out as she opened the door and slid in behind the wheel of her faded blue Civic.

Mitch leaned into the open door, one hand resting on the roof, the other on the back of her seat. ''I just don't want you to take any chances, Cass,'' he said softly.

''Damn it, Mitch,'' she snapped, staring up into eyes the color of the morning sky, ''if you want something badly enough, sometimes you've got to take a risk or two along the way.'' The words had come out before she'd had time to think how they'd sound, how she knew he'd take them. She felt a sharp pang of regret when she saw the flicker of pain in his eyes.

She groped for something to say to stave off the dark memories she'd triggered inside them both, memories still so vivid, not yet far enough past to forget.

''Cass...'' He seemed to want to speak to that past. To explain, to say something, anything that might break the barrier of pain and loss that wedged itself between them. ''You'd better get going,'' he said finally. ''I'll call you later.''

Cassie nodded, her throat too tight and too dry to speak.

''Take care,'' he said softly as he closed her door.

She watched him walk away, her heart throbbing, her eyes stinging. "Right," she whispered, drew a ragged breath, ran a shaky hand through her hair and slipped the key into the ignition. Take care, indeed. Between watching her back and watching her heart, Cassie knew she'd have her hands full.

"OOH, I LIKE IT! I really like it!" The high-pitched warble belonged to the petite lady under the huge magenta hat who'd stepped up into the window. "The *Nutcracker* has always been my favorite holiday event!"

"Good afternoon, Ms. Hahn," Cassie sputtered through teeth clamped down on half-a-dozen straight pins.

"Estelle, my dear," she corrected pleasantly. "Just plain old Estelle. Never stand on ceremony, I say. Cassie, this display is going to be utterly fantastic," she proclaimed, her arms outstretched to include the expanse of the unfinished holiday windows.

"I've still got a long way to go before opening night," Cassie explained, "but to tell the truth, I'm pretty pleased myself." She finished pinning a length of scarlet-colored velvet she planned to use for dramatic swags across each window. "But, thanks, Ms. Hahn—I mean, Estelle," Cassie managed with an awkward smile. Calling Grant Hahn's maiden aunt by her first name would take some getting used to. The woman was easily forty years Cassie's senior.

Estelle picked up a handful of the rich red velvet and ran a pale hand approvingly over the nap. "This will be perfect," she announced. "I have a feel for these things, my dear, I really do."

For a moment, her age melted away and Estelle Hahn looked like a child bursting with holiday fantasies and secret Christmas wishes.

"I thought it was the perfect shade, too," Cassie confided, smiling.

"You know," Estelle said, lowering her voice to a conspiratorial whisper, despite the fact that she and Cassie were the only ones in the display, "I'm planning to put in a good word for you with my nephew. I shouldn't be surprised if you had a very good chance to land the contract for the new store when it's completed."

Cassie knew the new store Estelle referred to was the one being planned at the Crystal Creek Mall site now under construction in the upscale south side area of the city. The latest Hahn venture was already being billed an ultrastore, the largest, most exclusive Hahn's ever. Landing that contract would be an incredible boost for Cassie and her newly formed business, High Country Designs.

She allowed herself a glimmer of optimism. Not only had Grant Hahn's aunt shown enthusiasm for her display ideas, but Lisa Hahn—Grant's pretty young wife whom Cassie had been introduced to the day her contract had been awarded—had seemed pleased, as well.

Although Lisa had dropped by the displays twice last week and expressed delighted approval, Cassie sensed it was Grant Hahn she'd need to impress in order to garner the contract for the Crystal Creek windows.

Though Grant had already promised her a trial run at the new store, Cassie knew better than to pin all her hopes on tomorrow—Mitch Dempsey had been a thorough teacher on the subject of broken promises, she reminded herself. Best to stick to the present, and make the most of the opportunity she'd been given here and now.

Estelle was eyeing the box of wooden soldiers delivered earlier that afternoon. "Would you like to take a peek," Cassie asked. The excited smile that blossomed on Estelle's face gave Cassie her answer.

"Oh, my dear, I'm such a snoop," Estelle admitted, her blue-gray eyes twinkling with delight. "But if you really wouldn't mind?"

"Not at all," Cassie said graciously. "I was planning to set them out before I left for the evening."

Cassie lifted the box up onto the worktable, and together they began unwrapping each individually packed soldier. It was easy to be generous to the likable and endearing Estelle Hahn. From her first day, Cassie had just naturally enjoyed the eccentric little lady in the outrageous hats who'd poked her cheery face around the corner of the display whenever she spied Cassie working.

Estelle, Cassie had learned from Arlene Crawford in cosmetics, loved to spend a couple of days a week at Hahn's, visiting with employees, lingering around the costume jewelry counters, inevitably trying on the newest hats and having a make-over—a freebie, of course—at the Elizabeth Arden counter.

For the most part, Arlene had confided, the staff found Estelle to be charming company. She did have a flair for drama, however, and sometimes her storytelling grew lengthy with embellishments and kept the staff from their regular duties or an impatient customer. Cassie had read between Arlene's carefully worded warning: Estelle Hahn, though eccentric and charming, could sometimes be an unwelcome pest.

Cassie remembered feeling a bit put out with Arlene for her less-than-loyal implications concerning the childlike Estelle. So far, the older woman hadn't interfered in the least with Cassie's work, and this evening her presence and friendly chatter created a welcome diversion from less pleasant thoughts of last night.

Already, in the short week since Cassie had met Estelle, she'd begun to feel the beginnings of a new friendship. Estelle's tales of her adventures as an amateur actress, starving artist and part-time costume designer fascinated Cassie.

It was a lengthy discourse on her background in high fashion that Estelle had launched into this evening. "I must have been no more than twenty-two, perhaps twenty-three when I managed to work my way to Paris. I studied with a woman infamous for her wretched temper. Madame Dupliese was her name, and as I soon came to discover, her reputation was well deserved."

Estelle's voice droned on and Cassie's attention wandered beyond the glass, her attention focused on the place where the stranger had been run down last night. She no longer heard what Estelle was saying as the awful events replayed in her mind's eye. The lights. The collision. The careening vehicle bearing down on her in the alley.

Cassie felt a pang of despair—for herself, for the stranger who had met with Lord only knows what terrible fate. To see people coming and going about the daily business of their lives with no knowledge of the drama that had taken place mere inches from where they now walked made Cassie's feelings of loneliness and despair multiply.

"Don't you agree, my dear?" Estelle's query cut across Cassie's bleak speculations.

She flushed with embarrassment. "Uh, excuse me?"

"I was just saying the styles of today are so much freer, less restricted, if you know what I mean. I find them . . ." Estelle's comments were cut short by the appearance of Arthur Lane's long, thin, humorless face at the entrance to the display.

"Ms. Craig, I'd like a word with you, please."

His voice was as stilted and formal as his attire. As Grant Hahn's assistant manager, Cassie guessed Arthur tried to achieve an image of authority, but the black three-piece suit he wore with the bloodred carnation in the lapel made the small-framed, narrow-shouldered Arthur Lane look like a pretentious maître d'.

"What can I do for you, Mr. Lane?" Cassie asked.

"I'm afraid you've already done it," he snapped as he stepped up into the display, a newspaper tucked firmly under one arm.

"Why, Estelle. Good evening. I hadn't expected to see you here," Arthur cooed with a flustered smile.

"Arthur." Estelle acknowledged him with a curt nod, obviously sharing none of his enthusiasm for their chance encounter. The icy edge Cassie noted in her newest friend's voice was unmistakable, as was the chilly detachment with which Estelle tolerated Arthur's hand assisting her down out of the display.

"See you tomorrow, my dear," Estelle promised Cassie with a reassuring smile. But that smile quickly faded. "Carry on, Arthur," she said over her shoulder as she left.

Cassie could almost feel the Hahn's manager bristle at Estelle's curt dismissal before he quickly turned his full attention, along with a disapproving glare, back to her.

"Ms. Craig, what is the meaning of this?" he demanded as he slapped a folded newspaper down onto the worktable in the center of the display.

Cassie glanced halfway down the page at the article encircled in glaring yellow highlighter—Hahn's Department Store Scene of Attempted Murder the headline read.

She snatched the paper up for a closer look. Scott Avery's article had been relegated to page twenty-six, and as he'd promised, it wasn't lengthy. The picture of Hahn's that accompanied the story took up nearly as much space.

But, as Cassie skimmed the contents of the article, she soon realized that in the short space he'd been given, the reporter had done everything he could to embellish and dramatize her story. She groaned inwardly.

Though the article never referred to her by name, Cassie realized to her horror that her anonymity had been severely compromised when Avery had written, "The unnamed witness was working as a decorator in the department store's windows when the accident took place." Cassie's stomach rolled.

For a moment, her hopes rose when she read on and saw that Avery had at least played down the value of the "unidentified" object found at the scene. But just as quickly, her hopes were dashed when she realized he'd managed to exploit that situation, as well, by referring to the "alleged witness" as the lucky finder of the object and the disappearing victim the hapless loser.

Cassie shook her head in stunned disbelief; she felt as though she'd been slapped.

"Well, Ms. Craig?" Arthur prodded. "What is your explanation for all of this? You were the 'alleged witness,' I presume?" He waited for an answer, his arms crossed tightly over his chest.

Cassie nodded numbly, her confused thoughts swirling as she groped for the right words, detesting the defensive position she felt she'd been forced to assume.

"You've read the article, Mr. Lane," she said softly. "I was working when I witnessed the...accident." The word *murder* slithered through her mind, but she couldn't bring herself to say it. Not yet.

She searched Arthur's grim expression for a flicker of compassion or understanding, but found neither.

"When I went to call for help...well, you read the rest." Cassie suppressed a shudder. "When I arrived home, the reporter from the *Herald* called me. I thought the article might encourage another witness to come forward."

"Hahn's does not need, or tolerate, this kind of negative publicity, Ms. Craig," he informed her.

"I'm sorry," she said honestly. "I had no idea there would be a picture or even a reference to the store." In fact, she hadn't even known for sure if there would *be* an article, she reminded herself. "I certainly didn't mean to cause any problems."

He stared at her as he rocked up onto the toes of his spit-shined shoes, a tiny muscle working convulsively in his jaw.

"I'm sorry," she said again. "I don't know what else I can say, Arthur."

"I suppose a small business such as High Country Designs can use all the free publicity it can get," he said cynically.

"What?" Cassie exclaimed, instantly outraged. "Publicity? Is that what you think this is all about?" All thought of any further apologies or explanations vanished as outright contempt flamed inside her. She'd done nothing wrong. How could she have known Scott Avery would play up the connection to Hahn's?

"It could be," Arthur replied unapologetically.

"I resent your implication, Mr. Lane," Cassie spat as she turned her back on him and grabbed her coat and purse. Feeling white-hot anger boiling inside, she feared if she didn't get away from the pompous assistant manager, she'd say something she'd live to regret later. "If you're finished with this little inquisition, I'll be going," she informed him as she brushed past him without waiting for his reply.

"Ms. Craig, you'd better listen to what I have to say," he warned, his voice shrill and threatening as he followed her out of the display.

Cassie whirled around to face him, her hands curled into fists at her side. "Mr. Lane, our conversation is over," she snapped.

"As will be your very short, very unsuccessful relationship with Hahn's if you persist on your present course, Ms. Craig," he warned.

His blatant threat of dismissal stopped her cold. Shocked, she could only stand staring into his cold eyes.

"Mr. Hahn abhors sensationalism," came the curt explanation. Arthur had lowered his voice in deference to their proximity to milling customers and employees on the sales floor. "In fact, Mr. Hahn doesn't wish to see his name in print at all except for the ads he personally approves."

Cassie nearly choked on the cloying aroma of his cologne as he moved closer. He dropped his voice another notch and added in a low, menacing tone, "It's all very simple, Ms. Craig, if you wish to complete the terms of your contract with Hahn's, say nothing further to the press."

"I hadn't planned to," she said tersely.

"Good," he sniffed, and with a satisfied smile, turned on his heel and left.

"The little worm," Estelle whispered as she appeared beside Cassie. Together they watched Arthur Lane stride away, smiling and nodding with practiced charm at each customer he encountered on his way to the elevator.

"Have you ever seen a more pathetic toupee?"

Cassie couldn't even force a smile. "Did you hear what he said?" she asked, swallowing her outrage to find her voice.

Estelle smiled sympathetically and patted Cassie's arm. "Enough to know I'd better have a little chat with Grant and see if I can smooth things over," she said. "Don't worry, my dear."

Cassie longed to feel relieved, but privately she wondered how much influence the aging aunt could possibly have on her young and powerful nephew.

"By the way," Estelle said brightly as they walked together across the first floor toward the north exit, "Lisa and I have been meaning to invite you to lunch. Share a little girl talk. How about tomorrow? Would twelve-thirty be convenient?"

Cassie nodded uncertainly. Would she be wined and dined and then dismissed?

"I'll call you later with directions. And now," Estelle said, her voice dropping to a whisper, "maybe you'd better go home and read the fine print on that contract of yours."

And that's exactly what Cassie planned to do. Right after she found a phone and shared a very large piece of her mind with one Scott Avery.

Chapter Four

"You fool! Did you read that newspaper article?" the voice on the other end of the line seethed. "She's found the keys! Do you understand what that means? Do you?"

The only reply was an uncertain silence.

"Rectify the situation immediately." The swift transition from near hysteria to deadly calm left the listener feeling unnerved.

"B-but how?"

"You figure it out," the caller barked savagely. "Find a way and find it fast. And I warn you, you'd better see to it that the job is done right this time. I've had enough of your bungling."

The reply was a whispered promise. "I know what I have to do and I'll do it." An iridescent trail of bluish smoke slid through thin lips. No one knew better. But would it be any easier the second time? Could one eventually learn to live with murder?

The answer to both questions—questions that nagged long after the caller hung up and the line went dead, was a resounding no.

IT WAS AFTER EIGHT when Cassie arrived home from
Hahn's, still shaken from her encounter with Arthur
Lane. Her senses took another jolt when she topped the
stairs to find Mitch leaning against her door, waiting
for her. At the sight of his welcoming smile, an odd
mixture of delight and apprehension rippled through
her.

"Now there's a woman who looks as though she
could use a home-cooked meal," he noted as she
opened the door. He followed her into the apartment
and went straight to the kitchen. "How about it?"

"Not tonight," she answered wearily. "I'm really
not very hungry." Trying to stabilize the effect Mitch
had on her emotional equilibrium wasn't easy. Just
how did one defend against a man whose presence was
both reassuring and comforting yet so thoroughly dis-
concerting and distracting at the same time? she wondered.

"Don't you ever buy groceries?" he asked her,
standing before the open door, surveying the meager
contents of her refrigerator.

"There's no point in rummaging through my
kitchen," she informed him. "I told you I wasn't hungry."

"Then how about a cup of Dempsey's special brew.
It's an old family recipe guaranteed to bring back your
appetite." His wry smile was disarming. The man could
make a root canal sound inviting, Cassie told herself.

"Sure, why not," she relented, knowing full well it
would take a good deal more than a cup of something
warm to dispel the chill that had for the past twenty-
four hours held her in its icy grip.

A gust of wind buffeted the glass doors behind her. Cassie pulled the pale blue curtains closed and dropped her coat over Samantha's arm as she punched the play button on her answering machine and listened to the message waiting there for her.

"Cassie, this is Scott Avery." Mitch and Cassie exhanged a dark glance. "Since I talked with you earlier, we've had a couple of calls concerning last night." The electronically recorded sound of Avery's voice filled the small apartment. "Both were cranks, I'm afraid. You know how it is, everybody wants a piece of the pie." His brittle laugh was dry and humorless. "If something substantial comes in, I'll let you know. Oh, hey, about that follow-up article, give it some more thought, and if you change your mind give me a call."

"Fat chance," Cassie exclaimed.

Mitch set two cups down onto the small round table and his grim expression gave way to a sympathetic smile. He didn't say a word, not even the "I told you so" Cassie figured must be choking him.

"Well, so much for the power of the press," Cassie muttered, dropping down into a chair. When she'd called Scott Avery before she'd left Hahn's, he'd firmly denied any intentional distortion of the facts or ulterior motives in using the photograph of the department store. When she'd grilled him for what she believed was a dead giveaway of her identity, he countered flatly that he had fulfilled his promise by withholding her name.

And when he'd asked if she would be interested in a follow-up article for next Sunday's edition, Cassie had hung up without giving him an answer. Again the anger and betrayal she'd felt rose to the surface.

"Drink your coffee," Mitch ordered gently.

Cassie sniffed suspiciously at the steaming contents of her cup. Judging from the pungent aroma that flirted with her nose, Mitch had put a decidedly Irish twist on the dark brew. Without warning, the distinctive smell evoked a memory of another wintery evening two years ago when she and Mitch had consumed one too many mugs of Irish coffee. Trying desperately to dull their pain after Brian's funeral, they'd soon discovered that nothing touched an ache that went all the way to the bone.

Cassie studied Mitch's face over the rim of her cup, half expecting and half afraid he'd shared her grim reverie.

"Remember these?" Mitch asked, jolting her with his choice of words. The keys made a jingling sound when he pulled them from his pocket and laid them down on the table.

"I thought about them all night," she replied, picking up the keys and examining them, as well as the small charm attached to the ring.

"I wasn't able to match the keys to any specific type of lock," he said.

Mitch pointed to the silver keys. "According to the locksmith, these two are probably just ordinary house keys, but he thought this third one was more unusual." He indicated the brass key marked Yale. "He said it could be an antique, possibly forty or fifty years old, or more."

"Another house key?"

Mitch shook his head. "It might be a house key, but the locksmith couldn't say for sure. I gathered from what he said that it's virtually impossible to tell one key from another unless there is some kind of identifying mark or special imprint stamped onto an individual key."

Cassie frowned as she leaned over the table and examined the keys more closely. None of these keys had any such identifying markings.

"What did he make of this?" Cassie asked, running her finger over the tiny front fender of the small gold charm attached to the key ring by a sturdy gold chain. "It almost looks like a token from a Monopoly game, doesn't it?" she added.

"It does at that," he agreed. "The locksmith guessed it might be a replica of a car from the twenties or thirties. By the way, you were right, it is fairly valuable."

Cassie's eyes posed the question.

"Solid gold. The jeweler I asked to appraise it assured me it's not the kind of trinket one could pick up at a discount store."

"Not the ones I frequent, anyway," Cassie said absently, her thoughts swirling. "You know, something tells me this little chunk of gold might provide us with some answers about its owner if only we knew what significance it held for him."

"I think you're right on target," Mitch said as he rose, walked across the room and picked up the large book he'd left on the side table beside the door when they'd come in.

"I was thinking the same thing, wondering what our little token might be able to tell us, so I stopped by the library on my way over tonight and picked up this. I don't really believe someone would have a solid gold replica of a car they merely admired."

Cassie joined him on the couch. Mitch opened the book entitled *Classic Automobiles* and balanced it between them.

"Maybe our mystery man is a car buff, a collector or even a dealer. Who knows? He might even own the real-life version of the model. I figure if we can identify the replica, discover the make and model, maybe we'll move a step closer to identifying its owner."

"And move a step closer to finding out what happened to him," Cassie added excitedly. "What a great idea!"

"Baby, I've got a million of them," he said, wiggling his dark eyebrows comically and flashing her a warm grin. When he took her hand and squeezed it, she couldn't help returning his smile. A rush of tenderness filled her.

His humor, his friendship, his touch—she'd missed them all so very much. She'd missed him, she admitted to herself. And for the first time in a long time, Cassie felt that inner chill beginning to thaw a bit.

FOR OVER AN HOUR they sipped Irish coffee and studied the color photographs of the antique cars that filled the pages of the large glossy coffee-table book. Finally Cassie spied a picture of a car that she thought looked especially similar to the small token that she'd stood on its four golden wheels on the table in front of them.

"Look at this," she said.

Mitch leaned closer, savoring the faintly floral scent of her perfume. "A Bentley," he said, picking up the key ring and holding the replica next to the page. "They do look similar. Yeah," he mused, "they really do. But look, see here? Something about the front end is different."

Cassie studied the car and the picture and finally nodded, her mouth set in a firm line of disappointment. As he watched her excitement fade, Mitch was seized with an almost overpowering urge to kiss that disappointment away.

"You're right," she agreed. "The hood of the Bentley is a bit different." With an exhausted sigh, she slapped the book closed, shoved it off her lap, leaned back against the cushions and closed her eyes.

"Let's call it a night," Mitch suggested. "Tomorrow we'll try again." She was exhausted. The events of the past forty-eight hours were beginning to take their toll. The faint shadows beneath her eyes attested to the strain she'd been under.

Mitch put his jacket on, and Cassie followed him to the door. "I guess we should keep at it," she said, sounding doubtful, "but I can't help wondering if any of this is doing any good. Even if we identify the car, what then?" she asked, sounding discouraged and weary.

He studied her, recalling how her eyes always took on a distinctly jade green color when she was tired. Impulsively he touched her cheek. His heart swelled when she didn't jerk away, but stood silently gazing back at him as though lost in her own private remembering.

"Cassie," he said gently, "we're going to do everything we can to get to the bottom of what you saw, I promise. It may seem to you as though we're taking the long way around, but we've got to work with what we have."

She nodded, her expression wistful, vulnerable and unguarded. It was an expression Mitch had seen a hundred times before and one that never failed to touch him. With every ounce of self-discipline he could muster he resisted pulling her into his arms and kissing her senseless. Instead, he merely brushed his lips lightly across her cheek, murmured a good-night and left.

FIVE MINUTES LATER, Mitch still sat in his car outside her building, gazing up at her window. He saw the lights in the living room go out and a soft glow appear in the bedroom window. With an inner groan, he quickly averted his gaze. Imagining Cassie getting ready for bed was an exercise in self-torture.

The problem was, these days almost all his thoughts centered on her. And torture was too mild a word for the intense feelings those thoughts evoked in him.

For the past two years, he'd tried to deal with her memory by immersing himself in the work for which he'd abandoned their personal future. Special assignments, marathon stakeouts and administrative overtime had helped. He'd been able to recover from the initial blow of Brian Shepard's death. He'd even been able to let go of the overwhelming feeling of grim responsibility.

But the memories of the life he'd forsaken with Cassie out of fear for their future lingered. At first, he'd tried to convince himself that his gut reaction had been a good one, that refusing to let Cassie make the sacrifices, take the risks that Holly Shepard had taken—that every cop's wife faced—had been the right thing for both of them. But in the end, he'd discovered there was nothing good or right about him and Cassie being apart.

So he'd tried calling her, but she'd refused to talk to him. He'd written her letters, but each one came back unopened. Finally last week, he put in for personal leave. His plan had been to go to New York and convince her to give their love another try. They'd be together again for Christmas, he'd promised himself.

But before he could put his plan into action, she was back in town and back in his life. He'd been given another chance. If he was ever going to win her over, reclaim their future, it was now or never, he told himself.

Sliding the keys into the ignition, Mitch gunned the Porsche to life. In a moment, he rounded the corner again and drove with headlights turned off down the deserted street. Before he reached her building, he killed the engine and rolled noiselessly up to the curb and parked on the opposite side of the street.

After a quick glance over at Cassie's darkened windows, Mitch reached for the metal thermos on the seat beside him and twisted the cap off. Winning Cassie back was his ultimate goal, he told himself as he poured the coffee, but for now, keeping her safe had to be his main concern.

For all her sophistication and intelligence, she was just too damn trusting. Anonymity was a fragile commodity. And whether Cassie knew it or not, that damned article in the *Herald* had shattered it for her, Mitch told himself angrily. But it was too late now to change what had already been done.

He'd planned on keeping a close eye on her anyway, Mitch reminded himself. The information revealed in the article would only make it a bit more inconvenient. Spending a few chilly nights in his car parked outside her building, sipping lukewarm coffee and fighting a charley horse now and then was a small price to pay for her safety.

Mitch had just taken another sip from the plastic cup when out of the corner of his eye, he caught a flash of movement across the street. The front door to Cassie's building was swinging closed. Someone had gone inside and he'd been so damn preoccupied that he hadn't seen who it was.

"Damn it," he blurted out as he wrenched open the car door, sprinted out onto the sidewalk and jogged across the street.

At the building, he jerked open the glass-and-metal doors and hurried inside. Peering down the first-floor hallway, he could see no one. The stairway below and the hallway that led to the apartments at garden level were deserted, as well.

At the opposite end of the long lower hallway, Mitch spied an outer door at the other end of the building. Whoever had come in might have had time to leave through that exit before Mitch had reached the building, but that possibility seemed unlikely.

A thudding sound above him jerked his attention to the second floor. Leaning over the railing, Mitch saw a woman, bent with age and walking with the aid of a heavy wooden cane emerging out onto the second-floor landing. She was a heavyset woman, bundled in a tattered gray coat with a woolen scarf tied snugly around her face and neck.

"Evening, ma'am," Mitch called out. "Did you just come in?"

The woman shifted two large brown bags whose handles were looped over her arm. "Why, yes, yes, I did," she said without turning around. "Is something the matter, young man?" Her tentative voice was edged with alarm.

Mitch regretted having frightened her. "No, ma'am," he reassured her quickly. "Everything's fine."

"Please be sure that front door is closed tightly, will you, young man?" she asked. "There's a terrible draft coming up the stairwell."

"Sure thing," Mitch said as he pushed open the main door and stepped back out into the night.

This thing has really got you jumping, Dempsey, he chided himself. The guys down at the station would have a heyday if they ever got wind that he'd taken to chasing down and scaring old ladies in the night.

Jogging over to the Porsche, Mitch allowed himself a small smile in the darkness as he slid behind the wheel and closed the car door. And what would Cassie say if she had any idea he'd camped outside her building for the night and was interrogating her neighbors as she slept? He could only guess at her exact words, but one thing he knew for sure: she'd be livid. Her fantastic green eyes would spark with righteous indignation.

For a moment, Mitch was lost in remembering how those eyes had once sparkled with passion and desire for him. Muttering a curse under his breath, he reached for the cup of coffee he'd abandoned. He scowled at the cold, bitter taste.

When he opened the door to toss out the offensive liquid, the sound of an alarm startled him. The electronic shriek was coming from Cassie's building and it split the night air and sent a rush of adrenaline surging through Mitch's body.

In a matter of seconds, he'd barked out the emergency call on the car phone and was out of the Porsche and across the street again.

The caustic smell hit him full force when he jerked open the apartment building's main door. A gauzy haze of smoke already filled the entryway, and Mitch had to blink back the stinging tears that sprang to his eyes.

As wide-eyed residents began to clamber out of their apartments, the air was filled with shouts, the sound of confused voices and the relentless scream of the fire alarm.

"The building is on fire," Mitch yelled. "Everyone stay calm, but get out!"

Mitch snatched up a crying child who stumbled to keep up with his mother, who clutched an infant cradled in her arms. Once the young woman and her children were safely out onto the sidewalk, Mitch ran back inside the building.

Thick smoke swirled up through the stairwell, curling and twining around the long smooth banister like ghostly fingers. Mitch took the stairs two at a time through the stinking haze.

Though he couldn't see flames yet—the smoke was so thick that he could hardly see anything—he knew he was getting closer to the source of the fire, and his heart pounded frantically against his chest. The air smelled more acrid on the second-floor landing, and the caustic stench bit at his lungs and throat with every breath.

Suddenly Mitch remembered the woman he'd seen on the stairs. Where was she? His burning eyes scanned the second-floor hallway, but as far as he could tell, it was empty. Had she managed to get out safely with the rest of the residents? Mitch didn't remember seeing her in the huddled crowd on the sidewalk.

Despite all the instincts that cried out for him to continue his trek to the third floor, to Cassie, he charged down the second-floor hallway, banging on doors, alerting anyone who might still be unaware of the danger. After he'd checked every apartment, Mitch ran back to the stairway.

For God's sake, where was Cassie? His desperate mind screamed the question as he continued his ascent to the third floor.

The alarm that penetrated the night with its blood-chilling electronic warning still screeched at full volume, and the sound reverberated through the smoke-filled hallways relentlessly, unnervingly.

"Cassie!" he shouted as he raced up the last stairs to the third floor. Once he reached the landing, only a deserted and smoke-filled hallway greeted him. Panic rose in his throat and he swallowed it.

By God, the thought of losing her was something he refused to let himself contemplate.

He raced down the hall to her apartment. Her door was closed but unlocked. An instant of blessed relief was overwhelmed by cold fear and numbing dread when he burst into her apartment only to discover it empty.

"Cassie!" he yelled as he raced from room to empty room. At the glass doors, he strained his eyes to find her among the crowd standing on the lawn, but he couldn't spot her.

Where was she, his frantic mind screamed. Where the hell was Cassie?

Chapter Five

When Mitch burst into the bathroom, he had to grab her to keep from sending her sprawling backward into the tub. She nearly doused him with the bucket of water that went flying from her hands, splattering the bathroom floor.

"Mitch!" Her cry was muffled by the wet washcloth she held over her mouth.

"Cassie!" Blessed relief flooded his senses at the sight of her. "You've got to get out of here," he yelled over the incessant wailing of the fire alarm.

"But the fire..." She choked.

He grabbed her arm as she reached for the bucket and shoved it under the faucet to fill it again. "We've got to get out," he insisted.

"The fire's in the hallway," she explained. "It's almost out. Hurry!"

Mitch grabbed the bucket and followed her out of the apartment. "There!" she shouted, pointing to the apartment next to hers where the flames skittered up the scorched doorway.

As he heaved the bucketful of water onto the flames, Cassie ran back into her apartment to fill another container. With their next watery assault the fire sizzled out, but not before belching another great gush of smoke out into the hallway.

"Come on," Mitch yelled, grabbing Cassie's hand and pulling her behind him toward the stairs. The fire was out, but the noxious fumes they'd been inhaling for the past several moments couldn't be doing either of them any good.

They met the firemen on the stairs. Mitch directed them to the third floor before ushering Cassie down the last few stairs and out of the building. In a moment, the fire alarm's chilling wail was at last silenced.

Cassie shuddered and Mitch saw that she was drenched to the skin. Shrugging out of his jacket, he draped it over her shoulders and led her across the street to the Porsche.

"Cassie, what happened up there?" he asked as he started the engine and flipped the heater switch on to high.

"I—I don't know," she stammered through chattering teeth. "I was in bed when I heard something out in the hallway. When I opened the door, I saw the flames."

"Cass," he murmured, pulling her into his arms. "Thank God, you're all right."

Fifteen minutes later, the firemen gave the dazed residents of the building permission to go back to their homes.

"Looks like something ignited a pile of rags outside your neighbor's door," the fireman in charge told Cassie. "That kind of fire puts out a bunch of smoke at first. We were lucky you got to it early, miss," he informed her. "You may have saved the whole building."

"I only acted on instinct," she said, dismissing his praise. She sighed. "Thank goodness 304 is vacant."

"Do you know how it started?" Mitch asked.

"Someone may have used lighter fluid or some other chemical to ignite the rags in a tin can," the fireman replied.

"In a tin can?" Cassie asked incredulously.

The fireman nodded. "We see this when the temperature drops. Street people wander into an unlocked building looking for a warm place to spend the night. Someone was probably just trying to get warm or cook themselves some sort of dinner. When the fire and smoke got out of hand, they must have panicked and run."

Mitch remembered the heavyset woman with the shopping bags on the stairs. "I saw someone inside the building just before the fire started." He described the woman to the fire chief.

"Sounds like one of our local bag ladies," the fireman said, shaking his head. "What they carry around would surprise you."

"This area does have its share of street people," Mitch said sadly, wishing now that he had offered the old woman some kind of assistance and wondering how she'd managed to get out of the building without him seeing her.

"Poor soul," Cassie said with a sigh. "She must have been desperate."

Mitch nodded; desperation was a feeling he'd experienced firsthand tonight when he'd thought for a few terrible moments that he'd lost the woman he loved.

THE NEXT MORNING Cassie was up before seven though the events of the harrowing night before made her long to pull the covers over her head and write the whole day off. But the fire last night had caused some smoke damage to her apartment and she'd decided to contend with it before she left for her lunch date at the Hahn mansion.

It was just after noon when Cassie turned off the narrow spruce-lined road and pulled up short in front of two formidable steel gates.

"This must be the place," she said to herself as she shoved the reluctant gearshift into neutral and firmly planted one foot on the brake. The little compact shuddered but didn't die, and for that Cassie was grateful. If the old bucket of bones stalled up here in Crystal Creek estates, she'd be forced to ask one of the resident millionaires to give her a push back down the hill.

Estelle had offered to send a car, but Cassie had declined the offer. If their friendly get-together turned into a not-so-friendly business confrontation, Cassie didn't want to be dependent on her employers for a way out of an unpleasant situation.

Rolling the window down, Cassie stared into the glossy black eye of a surveillance camera set into the massive stone pillar that supported one-half of the gate. It occurred to her that Grant Hahn had spent a small fortune on security systems for his home and his stores. Didn't anybody trust an old-fashioned lock and key anymore?

At the sound of the electronic buzz, the gates swung wide and Cassie eased her car through before they closed again, locking solidly behind her.

The light snow that had fallen last night had been scraped from the long, curving driveway, and in a moment, Cassie pulled up in front of the three-story mansion. Unblemished snow lay in gentle ivory folds like thick sugar frosting around the pink stone structure.

Cassie climbed out of the car and ascended the half-dozen stone steps that led up to the wide wraparound veranda. At the massive wooden door, she searched for a bell or buzzer. When she found none, she realized sheepishly that the electronic security system had already announced her arrival.

Half-expecting a tuxedoed butler when she heard a scuffing sound on the other side of the door, Cassie was relieved when it was Estelle's welcoming smile that greeted her.

"Cassie, dear, so glad you could make it," Estelle declared brightly. "Come in. Come in."

Estelle looped her arm through Cassie's and led her across the impressive marble foyer and down a wide paneled hallway that opened up into a sun-drenched atrium at the south end of the house.

Despite the glistening winter scene that lay beyond the glass, a profusion of blooming plants decorated the room, filling it with the vibrant colors and lively scents of summer. The only disagreeable element was the unmistakable odor of cigarette smoke wafting through the air.

Cassie wondered who in the Hahn household was a smoker and found her question immediately answered when she spotted Lisa Hahn crossing the room, holding a long, thin cigarette between fingertips that boasted nails that were a bit too long and a bit too pink for Cassie's personal tastes.

"So you managed to find us, huh?" Lisa smirked.

"The directions Estelle gave me were easy to follow."

"Good thing I didn't give them to you," Lisa quipped, "or you'd be wandering around in the mountains all day."

In the midday light that flooded the atrium, Lisa looked even younger than Cassie had remembered. That first day at Hahn's, she'd guessed that Lisa was close to her own age. But today, dressed in pink stirrup pants and a bright patterned sweater, Lisa could have passed for a college student. The profusion of frosted blond curls that framed her pretty face accentuated her youthful look.

"Your home is lovely," Cassie said as Estelle took her coat.

"It is something, isn't it?" Lisa agreed.

The meal awaiting them on a glass-topped wicker table laid with shimmering crystal and gleaming silver was a delicious-looking and colorful assortment of fruit, vegetables, meats and cheeses.

"You've met my husband's secretary, Ruth Palmer, I guess." Lisa nodded at the attractive, well-dressed brunette standing near the French doors.

"Of course," Cassie said. "Nice to see you again, Ruth." She remembered meeting Ruth Palmer for the first time when she'd signed the display contract in Grant Hahn's office. At that first meeting, Cassie had come away with the impression that Ruth was the official watchdog of the executive offices. Later, Arlene had reinforced that impression by confiding that Grant Hahn's personal secretary was quite proud of her protective image and did everything to enhance it.

"How are you, Ms. Craig?" Ruth inquired, her cool smile polite and professional.

"Please, call me Cassie."

Ruth nodded without disturbing a single strand of the sleek chignon she wore at her nape.

"Sit down, everybody," Lisa urged, motioning Cassie into the chair next to her. "I'm starving." As she poured the wine for her guests, Lisa continually sipped from her own glass.

The conversation during lunch was light. Other than an occasional reference to the Crystal Creek Mall development, Cassie sensed that the three women deliberately steered the conversation away from business. When the table was cleared by a uniformed maid, Estelle offered coffee. As Estelle poured, Lisa refilled her wineglass.

"Tell me about Sunday night, Cassie," Lisa blurted. The abrupt request seemed to come from out of nowhere.

"It must have been just awful for you, my dear," Estelle added. "The article in the *Herald* was gruesome," she declared with a shudder. "I don't know how you kept your wits about you. I think I would have fainted dead away.''

Lisa laughed loudly and Cassie managed a weak smile.

"There was quite a bit of confusion surrounding the incident, wasn't there? Something about a disappearing body or something like that?'' Ruth asked, leveling her gaze on Cassie over the rim of her cup.

"Yes,'' Cassie replied, her voice shaky. "The victim was gone by the time the ambulance arrived.''

"But the important thing is that the whole unpleasant incident is behind you,'' Ruth concluded.

"It's almost as if someone were playing a dirty trick on you, isn't it? You know, like a practical joke or something,'' Lisa suggested.

Her implication shocked Cassie. "I can assure you, Lisa, what happened was no joke,'' she said firmly. "And nothing is really over until they discover what happened to the victim,'' she added for Ruth's benefit. The "incident,'' as Ruth had so impersonally termed it, involved a flesh-and-blood individual and an all-too-real attempt on her own life. Nothing would be over until the driver was caught and brought to justice, she reminded herself grimly.

"My dear,'' Estelle said, patting Cassie's hand gently, "you must think us terribly insensitive. My goodness, how traumatic all of this must be for you!''

"Yes,'' Ruth put in quickly. "It must have been very difficult for you when the police refused to believe your story.''

The momentary silence crackled.

"Ladies," Estelle said at last, "perhaps Cassie would rather not discuss this. I'm sure her only thought is to put the whole unpleasant affair behind her as quickly as possible and move forward toward the holidays."

Cassie felt three sets of eyes turn expectantly toward her.

"Estelle is right." Lisa said brightly. "The whole thing should be dropped, and the sooner the better."

Cassie felt the anger bubbling up inside her. "Estelle. Lisa. Thank you for lunch," she said quickly, reaching for her purse. "But I think I'd better be going." Though she fought to control it, her anger put a quiver in her voice. "If this little get-together was designed to convince me that I merely imagined what I *know* I saw, and what I *know* happened to me in that alley, then I'm afraid you've wasted your time. Arthur Lane tried to do the same thing, and I can assure you it didn't work for him, either."

The floor felt as though it were tilting as Cassie rose and walked across the room. At the door, she felt a hand on her sleeve.

"Please, Cassie," Lisa implored, "don't leave. I apologize if it felt as though we were ganging up on you. And as for Arthur, well, he can be such a jerk. But we really didn't mean to upset you."

"You must believe that," Estelle added breathlessly.

Ruth, her expression stony, nodded her agreement.

"If you'll give me the chance, maybe I can explain my husband's dislike for the press," Lisa said.

"Please," Estelle chimed in, "just hear her out."

Cassie looked from one woman to the other. Curiosity fought with her disdain of pretense and manipulation—practices she despised and felt both Lisa and Estelle and probably Ruth had conspired in by inviting her to lunch.

In the end, Cassie's practical side prevailed. There was too much at stake to walk away without hearing them out. After all, her future and the future of the heavily indebted High Country Designs rested on the Hahn account and similar accounts in the future.

She cast a wary look between Estelle and Lisa. The older woman wore the innocent expression of a confused child, completely without guile. Lisa's large blue eyes were pleading.

"I'll stay and listen to what you have to say, but only for another cup of coffee, then I really have to get back to the store."

"Wonderful!" Estelle exclaimed, clasping her hands together in a silent clap. Turning to her nephew's wife, she chirped, "Didn't I tell you everything would work out?"

Lisa told the maid to bring fresh coffee and to see to it they weren't disturbed. Cassie settled into her chair, telling herself that she'd been wise to stay. If there really was some reason why the Hahn family was intent on covering up the events of Sunday night, she was dying to hear what it was.

"I was born in New Mexico," Lisa began. "Most of my life I spent in and out of foster and group homes."

None of them very pleasant, Cassie guessed, watching the pain flicker in Lisa's eyes as she reached again for the ever-present bottle of wine.

"Anyone care to join me?" Lisa offered. Ruth and Estelle shook their heads.

"No, thanks," Cassie said, covering the top of her glass with her hand.

Lisa shrugged and poured the last of the wine into her own glass. As if on cue, the maid reappeared just long enough to uncork a fresh bottle and slip it into the sterling ice bucket at her employer's elbow.

"My mother was a fifteen-year-old runaway," Lisa continued as soon as the maid left the room. "Although she couldn't bring herself to give me up for adoption, she couldn't find a way to keep me with her, either."

With eyes downcast, Lisa traced a translucent bead of moisture down the stem of her glass with one long, pink nail.

"I had no father," she said softly. "That is, his name was never mentioned."

Estelle's expression was sympathetic. Ruth fidgeted nervously in her seat. Cassie listened with compassion but couldn't help wondering why Lisa Hahn, a virtual stranger, not to mention her employer's wife, chose to divulge the details of what had to be extremely painful memories from her unhappy past.

Lisa fumbled to retrieve a cigarette from a small porcelain box sitting beside her on the table. "Mind?" she asked, giving her guests a cursory glance.

Ruth scowled, but Cassie merely shook her head. She knew the cigarette smoke would produce a dull headache later, but it made little difference at this point; Lisa had been smoking steadily for the past hour.

"Do go on, dear," Estelle urged. "Finish your story. It's common knowledge, anyway," she confided to Cassie.

Lisa stared at Estelle for a long moment. If some emotion other than indifference was lurking behind her gaze, Cassie didn't see it.

"At seventeen, I had a baby of my own to support and no husband." Her words were beginning to slur into each other. "I landed a job at Hahn's in Albuquerque." She jutted her chin defiantly. "I met Grant six months later and inside of eight weeks, we were married."

Cassie caught a glimpse of the hard frown that drove deep, unattractive lines around Ruth Palmer's small mouth. At the same moment, an odd smile curved Lisa's lips.

"As you can imagine, I wasn't exactly what the members of Denver's social set had in mind as the perfect match for their most handsome, most eligible bachelor."

Lisa gazed vacantly at Cassie and her quirky smile faded.

Cassie shifted in her chair, feeling increasingly uncomfortable with Lisa's silence. Her movement seemed to pull Lisa back to the present.

"Needless to say," Lisa drawled cynically, "the press had a field day uncovering the lowlife background of Grant Hahn's new bride."

Ruth shook her head and said softly, "It was a very difficult time for Grant."

"For all of us," Lisa snapped, her voice bitter. "But my husband is a very proud man. Always the proper gentleman, you know. Even if he felt he'd made the biggest mistake of his life, he'd never admit it to anyone," she grumbled, her words punctuated with a sardonic smile as she pressed the rim of her wineglass to her lips and drained it.

"But, of course, he never believed that for one moment," Estelle put in quickly.

Lisa nodded lazily. "Of course not."

There was pride in Estelle's voice when she announced, "My nephew has yet to reconcile with the press or many of those so-called friends who chose to snub Lisa."

Cassie felt her uneasiness growing steadily. What on earth did any of this have to do with her? Why had Lisa launched into these frank disclosures? Was she trying to warn or threaten, or had consuming too much alcohol simply caused her to reveal what tomorrow she'd regret having mentioned?

"He still refuses to run any ads in the *Herald,*" Ruth said, tugging Cassie away from her private speculations.

Lisa rose and moved awkwardly around behind Estelle's chair. Resting her hands heavily on the older woman's shoulders, she continued, "Grant and I weren't the only ones put through the wringer," she said. "Estelle was hurt by all that media crap, too."

Cassie nodded, a simple gesture of understanding that belied the embarrassed confusion she felt swirling inside.

"Good, I'm glad you get it," Lisa said, her tone stronger. "It's settled and we understand each other," she announced, smiling as she plopped back down into

her chair and brought her glass to her lips trium-
phantly. "Didn't I tell you two she'd listen, that between us girls we could get this whole damn hit-and-run
thing settled?"

Hit-and-run thing? Settled? Cassie's startled mind
blurted. "Lisa, I know it must have been very difficult
for you to relive the things you've shared with me this
afternoon," she began, grappling for the right words.
"And I want you to know I sympathize with what
you've gone through—I really do." In the past twenty-
four hours, Cassie had learned firsthand how even a
small distortion of the facts by the media could ad-
versely affect one's life.

"It must have been a terrible time...for all of you.
But I can't see how the crime I witnessed or my agreeing to be interviewed by the *Herald* has anything to do
with you or with Hahn's. What I saw just happened to
take place in front of your store. Other than that, I
can't see any connection to you or your husband at
all."

Lisa's eyes snapped and her lips shriveled into a tight
frown that made her pretty face look years older and
several degrees colder than Cassie would have thought
possible.

Estelle's expression was one of open anxiety as she
avoided Cassie's eyes by fidgeting with an invisible
piece of loose string at the hem of her blue silk dress.
Ruth's expression was impassive and unreadable. For
a long moment no one spoke. The air in the atrium felt
hot and stuffy, and a dull pounding had started behind Cassie's eyes.

"Mrs. Hahn?" The brittle silence was suddenly and blessedly broken when the maid reentered the room.

Lisa didn't look up. "What do you want, Patty?" she snapped.

"It's nearly two." Patty's reply was tentative. "You told me to remind you. Brandon will be home from school soon, and your counseling session is scheduled for three."

"Fine," Lisa growled. She bumped into the table when she got up out of her chair and staggered when she walked across the room. Cassie wondered how someone who'd consumed as much alcohol as Lisa had in the past hour could possibly attend any sort of meeting.

At the door, Lisa turned and locked a glassy, emotionless stare on Cassie. "You'd better think twice before you go running back to the press, Ms. Craig."

Running to the press? Ms. Craig? The chill in the air couldn't have been colder if Lisa had raised a window and let the winter wind blow through. "I will think about what you said," Cassie retorted, rising quickly from her own chair. "Thank you for inviting me to lunch—" she found herself unable to resist adding a pointed "—*Mrs. Hahn.*"

Lisa nodded absently before swaying out the door.

"I'd better be getting back to the office," Ruth said stiffly as she reached for her purse. "Nice to see you again, Estelle. Cassie, I'll see you at work."

"Goodbye, Ruth," Estelle called after her as Ruth strode briskly past them.

"Brandon is Lydia's son," Estelle supplied as Cassie reached for her jacket and bag. "He's only eight years old, but he acts so grown-up sometimes. He's such a good little boy."

Cassie nodded politely as she, too, prepared to leave. She felt sympathy for Estelle, trying to pick up the pieces of the difficult luncheon, and pity for the child coming home to find his mother as drunk and as obviously ill-humored as Lisa Hahn had been when she'd left the room.

"My dear," Estelle said, following Cassie down the hall and into the foyer. "I'm so sorry. Lisa is a good person, really she is," she insisted. "But I'm afraid she's never quite got over the social snubbing she received when Grant brought her back to Denver. If only you could try to understand." Estelle's kind eyes were pleading.

"I am trying," Cassie said with an exasperated sigh at the front door. "Look, none of this is your fault, Estelle. You were only trying to help, but I just fail to see what any of this has to do with me."

Estelle crooked her finger, motioning Cassie to follow her back into the hallway as if she were about to impart a secret vital to national security.

"Their wedding was a truly dismal affair," Estelle confided in a whisper. "Two weeks later, Lisa was taken to the hospital, where she miscarried." Estelle's voice had dropped a disapproving notch.

"When it was discovered that Lisa would never be able to conceive again, the gossip mongers attacked with renewed fervor, speculating on how long Grant would remain married, since the pregnancy that had obviously prompted the marriage had ended in disaster."

"That's awful!" Cassie exclaimed.

Estelle gave a grim nod. "Grant immediately made arrangements to adopt little Brandon. He cares about that child as if he were truly his own," Estelle proclaimed, her voice rising with pride. "But two days before the adoption was scheduled to take place, Brandon was kidnapped."

"Dear God!" It seemed to Cassie that with each disclosure the Hahn family past seemed more filled with tragedy.

"The little guy was snatched right out of his bed, right out of this very house," Estelle explained dramatically. "Grant paid the ransom, of course, and a few days later Brandon was found blessedly unharmed. But the kidnappers were never apprehended and the money was never recovered."

As Estelle had recounted the details, Cassie remembered having heard or read something about the kidnap case several years ago.

"And once again the tabloids sensationalized the tragic events surrounding the Hahn family, I suppose."

"Yes." Estelle nodded sadly. "It was a terrible time. Grant threw himself with renewed fervor into making Hahn's the incredible success that it is. And Lisa... well, she found other ways to relieve her pain... alcohol, pills..."

Estelle followed Cassie back into the foyer, casting a wary eye in all directions as she spoke. "Now maybe you can see why the picture of Hahn's in the *Herald* caused such a stir."

"I guess I do," Cassie admitted. "And I appreciate you telling me. But surely you can see how I just can't forget what I saw, pretend it never happened?"

Estelle shook her head, her expression one of weary defeat. "No," she said solemnly. "I don't suppose you can."

"I just can't," Cassie reiterated, the memory of what she'd seen and what she'd been through Sunday night tightening like a knot around her heart. Even as she spoke, Cassie felt a new resolve lodging itself deeply inside her, surprising in its intensity.

Estelle's face had grown pale. "Look," Cassie said, touching the older woman's arm reassuringly. "I'm sorry I've upset you. I'm sorry *anyone* is upset," she added frankly. "And I assure you I won't be talking to the *Herald,* again," she promised. Scott Avery's article certainly hadn't produced the results she'd hoped for. The prank calls that had come into the *Herald* office had convinced Cassie that trying to find a witness or the stranger through the news article was hopeless. Mitch had been right; the article had produced only turmoil.

"Thank you," Estelle said earnestly, her soft eyes shimmering. "I'll tell Grant this evening. He'll be so pleased the matter is settled."

But a few moments later, as Cassie turned onto the main road and headed back to work, Estelle's parting words echoed in her mind, and she knew that for her the matter was far from settled.

Lost in thought, Cassie had traveled almost a mile before she noticed the black limousine hovering uncomfortably close behind her. She sped up, and when she glanced again in the rearview mirror, the long sleek vehicle was pulling out to pass her.

Cassie's gaze flicked back to the road and she gasped in horror. Up ahead, where the narrow road curved sharply down a steep incline, a small red sports car was coming toward them up the hill. A head-on collision was inevitable.

Cassie's startled mind grasped the situation with a shriek. Instinctively she wrenched the steering wheel to the right and stomped down on the brake. The Honda skidded to a stop on the snowy shoulder. The limousine sped past, missing the sports car by mere inches.

For a few minutes after both cars had disappeared, Cassie sat trembling behind the wheel, imagining what might have happened had she failed to see the sports car in time. She felt shaken, and it took several deep breaths before she felt steady enough to pull back out onto the road.

The driver of the limousine had to be crazy or drunk to have taken such a dangerous risk. The latter was more likely, Cassie told herself with grim certainty, remembering the glimpse she'd caught of the personalized license plate on the sleek limousine that read, Hahn 1.

CASSIE WAS EXHAUSTED by the time she had finished the displays for the night. She'd had to force herself to stop for some basic essentials at the grocery store on her way home. It was well after nine when she finally trudged up the stairs toward her apartment and heard the sound of footsteps on the landing above her. The image of Mitch waiting at her door slipped easily into her mind.

Her heart broke into a staccato beat. It happened every time, Cassie admitted to herself as she shifted the bag of groceries and quickened her pace. Thoughts of the familiar grin she hoped would be waiting made her smile.

But instead of seeing Mitch when she stepped out onto the third-floor landing, Cassie saw only a blur of blue heading straight for her. Instinctively she grasped the railing and tried to step aside, but the hallway was too narrow.

A startled breath caught painfully in her throat as the bone-jarring impact sent her reeling backward, the bag of groceries flying from her grasp. She squeezed her eyes against the sharp pain in her ribs, and when she opened them again she saw the back of someone dressed in a blue nylon jacket and a black baseball cap racing down the stairs.

"Hey! Hey, you. Stop!" Cassie shouted as she raced after the person who'd nearly sent her down three stories through the open stairwell.

On the second-floor landing, Cassie heard the front door clanking closed, and a gust of cold air told her he had gone. A moment later with her heart pounding, Cassie stood at the front door, peering out into the street. Whoever had crashed into her had disappeared into the darkness.

"Kids," she muttered as she trudged back up the stairs, collecting her scattered groceries as she went. Anger dissolved into trepidation when Cassie reached the third floor again and saw her door standing wide open.

The ominous and very real possibility that whoever had slammed into her on the landing had been on his way out of her apartment caused the skin on the back of her neck to prickle.

Clutching her groceries tighter, Cassie moved cautiously down the hallway. At her door, she stopped a moment, scanning the apartment's interior without stepping inside. Everything looked exactly as she remembered leaving it. But the idea of an intruder having been there certainly made everything feel different. Very different and very frightening.

Setting the groceries down, she glanced at the apartment next door and remembered it was vacant. Her other neighbor, Lucille Mendoza, lived at the end of the hall in 306, but she'd left town Saturday. Cassie had promised to look after her canary, Caruso, while she was away. Walking quickly toward Lucille's apartment, Cassie pawed through her purse, trying to find the keys Lucille had left with her.

"Great, just great," she groaned, remembering the keys were in her own apartment. She'd hung them on the peg beside the phone in the kitchen to remind her to check on Caruso every day.

Cassie glanced back at her own apartment nervously. There's no one in there now, she told herself. Just go inside and call Mitch. The thought startled her. "Go inside and call the *police*," she corrected aloud.

A creaking sound on the stairs propelled Cassie into decisive action. She bolted through the door seconds before a long shadow slid up the last three stairs and into the hallway.

With panic choking her, Cassie threw her shoulder against the door, trying desperately to close and lock it. Stark terror gripped her as a determined and much stronger force on the other side shoved against her. A shattering scream sliced her throat as the ominous force on the other side of the door broke through.

Chapter Six

"For God's sakes, Cass!" Mitch shouted as he shoved the door open wide. "What is it?"

She stood staring back at him, unable to hear a word over the deafening pounding in her chest and the wave of relief cresting over her stunned senses.

"Mitch?" she whispered as the blood drained from her face and her knees went wobbly. She didn't fight him when he pulled her into his arms.

"Cass." He whispered her name against her cheek as he moved them deeper into the room and closed the door. "What the hell's going on?"

"I thought he was back, Mitch," Cassie said, her voice trembling as she drew a ragged breath and clung to him. "I—I thought he'd come back."

"Who?" Mitch asked, reluctantly holding her at arm's length and looking into the green eyes wide with fright and staring past him.

"Down there!" she gasped, moving to the glass doors. "Do you see him?"

A man wearing a black cap stood on the street below. When he glanced up at them, Cassie grabbed

Mitch's arm and backed them both away from the glass.

"Damn it, Cassie, what's going on? Who is that guy?"

"He crashed into me on the stairs a few minutes ago."

Mitch frowned.

"My door was standing wide open when I got home. That's why you nearly gave me heart failure when you came barging in here a few minutes ago...."

Mitch was out the door and down the stairs, leaving Cassie to finish her sentence to the empty room.

"Wait!" she called after him as she hurried out onto the landing and peered over the railing. "I'm going with you."

He didn't look up. "Stay there." His shouted order was an authoritative bark that echoed through the narrow stairwell, landing disagreeably on Cassie's senses.

"No way, Detective Dempsey," she muttered as she took the stairs two at a time trying to catch up. Even if the man she'd seen from the window hadn't broken into her apartment, and even if there was some other explanation for the open door, she'd still have plenty to say to someone who'd slammed into her and run off without an apology.

A hit and run, she thought, the grim phrase popping unbidden into her mind.

When she reached the front door and stepped out into the night, she saw Mitch racing down the street. She ran after him, and in a few moments she caught up to him at the alley halfway down the block.

Mitch jogged over to her, shaking his head. "He must have spotted us in the window. By the time I got down to the street, he'd taken off. I thought I saw someone turn down this alley, but by the time I got here, he was gone."

Cassie shivered. When he wrapped his arms around her, she leaned into his warmth, borrowing the strength she hoped would penetrate the unnerving feeling of vulnerability that seemed to have penetrated through to her bones.

"Let's go in," Mitch said, guiding her back inside the building.

Once upstairs, he examined the lock.

"Do you think he was in here?" Cassie asked.

"I'm not sure," he said uneasily. "The lock doesn't appear to have been tampered with." But he picked up the phone and called the police and a locksmith, anyway.

"Take a look around," he said. Placing one hand over the mouthpiece, he added, "But don't touch anything."

Cassie suppressed a fresh wave of shivers. Though everything looked the same, the sense of security, the cozy warmth she'd felt from the very first day in her apartment home had turned to cold uncertainty. Even the air somehow felt different, Cassie thought. Smelled different, too. Was it cigarette smoke she detected lingering in the air?

As she listened to Mitch give the locksmith her address, she glanced at her TV, VCR and stereo system still lodged snugly inside the antique wardrobe she'd converted into an entertainment center. Her gaze swept the living room again, taking in the furniture pieces she'd chosen more for individual charm and aesthetic appeal than actual monetary value.

"What went on here tonight, Sam?" she asked the stoic mannequin. Cassie wished tonight, as she had more than once in the past, that her cool-eyed, unblinking friend could talk.

When Mitch hung up the phone, he followed Cassie into the kitchen, where they found each cupboard door gaping open. Cassie noticed that Lucille's keys were no longer hanging on the peg beside the wall phone. In her panic, she must have overlooked them in her purse, she told herself.

"Now what could a burglar possibly want in my kitchen?" Cassie asked.

Mitch shrugged. "The man was obviously *not* a gourmet." His frown melted into an knowing smile.

Despite being the target of his dumb joke, Cassie felt a wave of relief and coaxed a smile of her own. She was feeling more grateful by the moment that Mitch was here, and it was a feeling that went far beyond the need for her immediate physical safety.

He caught her hand when she reached for a cupboard door, and held it gently. "Don't," he said. "Fingerprints, remember? As soon as the lab boys leave, I promise I'll make us something terrific for dinner."

Her heart did a tiny flip as he squeezed her hand gently. "She says she's forgotten me, Sam," he said, playfully directing his comments to the mannequin across the room, "but I know she hasn't forgotten my western omelets."

A flood of color rose to Cassie cheeks at the mention of their favorite "morning after" breakfast and the sensuous memories it evoked.

"Right," Cassie said, trying to sound cynical as she jerked her hand away from his and backed out of the room. It wasn't just their lovemaking memories that chased her out of the kitchen, Cassie admitted to herself. The room was beginning to feel as if it were closing in on her. With its yawning cupboard doors as physical proof, the break-in was beginning to feel like a personal violation.

Cassie allowed herself a small measure of cautious optimism as she stepped into her bedroom and didn't immediately notice anything out of place. But the thought was comforting only for a moment.

Perhaps the intruder had found what he wanted in the kitchen. But what? Lucille's apartment keys? Or maybe he'd only started his search in the kitchen and when he'd heard her on the stairs he'd taken flight.

An uneasy feeling of nameless fear gnawed at her as she emptied the contents of her jewelry chest onto the bed. Except for the emerald earrings that had been her grandmother's, the diamond pendant given to her by her parents and a pair of pearl earrings she'd purchased for herself in New York, Cassie didn't own any really valuable jewelry.

These few pieces, along with a large variety of colorful costume jewelry, were all accounted for.

"All there?" Mitch asked from the doorway.

"I think so. There's a pair of earrings—inexpensive gold hoops missing, but I've probably just mislaid them."

"Good."

Cassie nodded but admitted to herself that she might feel better if something *had* been taken. A garden variety break-in she could handle, but this didn't make sense. The vagueness, the not knowing frightened her to the core.

As she began to gather up the jewelry strewn across her rose-colored bedspread, Mitch reached over and picked up a small black velvet jeweler's box that had rolled against the pillows.

"Don't forget this," he said, his voice betraying no emotion.

Cassie felt her pulse quicken as she grabbed the small box and slipped it into the larger case without looking up. It may have been cowardly, but at that moment Cassie felt as if making direct contact with Mitch's gaze would spell emotional disaster.

"Don't you think you ought to at least check to see if it's still in there?" he said quietly.

She felt the heat of his steady gaze on her as she withdrew the ring box again. The picture of a shimmering diamond mounted on a band of twisted antique gold formed in Cassie's mind even before she raised the small hinged lid.

He was right, of course. She had to see if her engagement ring was still there. *His ring,* she made the mental correction. In her mind, the ring had ceased to belong to her the moment he'd broken their engagement. Despite her insistence two years ago, he'd refused to take it back. She'd tried again to return it just before she'd left for New York, but still he'd refused.

When Cassie found she couldn't bring herself to return the custom piece to the goldsmith who'd designed it for them, she'd stashed it away in the back of her jewelry box, vowing that once she got settled in New York she would place it in a safe-deposit box.

But two years had come and gone, and somehow she'd never brought herself to make that special arrangement at the bank.

Now, taking a deep breath, she flipped open the lid quickly and stared down at the ring. A wave of bittersweet relief broke over her. The precious band that still represented so much of what had once been the best part of her life was safe. Cassie admitted to herself that she was very glad it was.

"Does it still fit?" he asked, sitting down beside her close enough for their shoulders to touch.

"I wouldn't know," Cassie said sharply, still avoiding the perceptive eyes that had always been able to detect her lies.

"Not even curious?"

"I'm sure my ring size hasn't changed, despite the pound or two I've added in other places." The lighthearted tone she'd tried to achieve fell flatly between them.

"I haven't noticed any changes." His voice was a satiny thread tugging at her heart. "You're as beautiful and sexy as ever, Cass."

She stiffened and sat up straight, fighting the rush of emotion his unabashed flattery sent coursing through her. Even as she simmered, she knew it would take a good deal more than a stiff spine to protect her from her one fatal weakness—Mitch Dempsey's charm.

"Some changes are easier to see than others. But believe me they're there," she informed him, snapping the lid closed and picking up a tangled gold chain. Focusing her attentions on working out the knot kept her eyes occupied.

He touched her chin and gently forced her to look at him. Stubbornly she kept her eyes lowered, anger and confusion fighting for possession of her emotions. At last lifesaving, pride-saving anger won out, and she tossed the chain aside and glared at him defiantly.

If merely staring into those baby blues would cause the sky to fall, she'd find out sooner of later. If two years, two thousand miles and at least a million tears hadn't had some effect on her Mitch Dempsey defense system, nothing ever would. Damn it all, she might as well find out now.

"Things *have* changed, Mitch," she blurted, finding a surprising strength in her voice as she glared at him. "And despite what your overinflated ego might tell you, it'll take a hell of a lot more than a few scrambled eggs, a sexy smile and a slick compliment to make things right again." Crossing her arms protectively over her heart, she took a deep breath and braced for his retort.

He did exactly what she should have known he'd do. He smiled. "Okay," he drawled, nodding agreeably. "I'll buy that. So tell me. What will it take, Cassie? What will it take to make you love me again?"

She felt the familiar flutter in her chest and cursed the way she'd set herself up. "You're impossible," she snapped. "You won't even admit it when you know I'm right."

"But I will." He grinned. "And you are. Right, that is. At least about things changing," he said softly, his smile fading like the sun slipping behind the mountains at dusk.

Without warning, he took both her hands in his and brought them slowly to his lips. His movements were slow, deliberate and maddeningly hypnotic. His steady blue gaze held her motionless.

"I've changed," he said, his expression growing so darkly intense that just one look made Cassie's heart constrict achingly in her chest.

"I only hope I'll have the chance to show you just how much," he said in a gruff whisper.

Her defenses screamed for her to pull away. She couldn't afford to believe him. She'd believed him before and paid the price. But as his lips began to caress each tingling fingertip, Cassie's defenses melted like butter on a hot griddle.

"Mitch." His name was a weak protest that perished on her lips as he pulled her close. Her anger was washed away in one long wave of sweet, warm desire. In the next heartbeat, his mouth covered hers.

The strange events of the evening were forgotten. The past and the future became empty concepts without meaning. For Cassie, the only reality was the current of desire she felt rushing between them, growing stronger, more intense by the moment.

Slumbering physical sensations awoke with a start when he held her, touched her, kissed her as she'd yearned for him to hold, touch and kiss her for so long. Too long.

Everything would be all right again, her heart insisted, as long as he never let her go. They were together again, and that was all that mattered. Together again, at last.

The heat of his urgent kisses ignited a burst of mindless pleasure inside her and Cassie's lips began their own desperate seeking and tasting, a hungry reacquainting of appetites too long denied.

In a low seductive murmur she heard him speak her name. But as he pulled her down beside him onto the bed, another sound slipped through the veil of her desire, tugging her from the spell under which she had so willingly fallen captive. It was the sound of her own voice, a deep sensual moan coming from the back of her throat, that frightened her back to the real world and saved her from the fall—a fall from which she might not recover this time, her common sense warned in one last desperate shout.

"No!" she gasped, wrenching out of his arms, feeling as though a part of her heart were being torn away as she did. "This is crazy," she cried. An ache lodged inside her as his arms fell away and she found herself immediately grieving the loss.

"It's the only sane thing we've done in two years," Mitch insisted, his voice a low growl, his blue-eyed gaze still heavy with desire.

She stood up and moved away from him and the bed. Her best arguments stuck in her throat as she battled the desperate need to ignore her head and lead with her yearning heart.

He stood up and moved toward her. She held her breath when he reached out and touched her hand and looked into her eyes.

"Cass, don't try to tell me you don't still care. I could feel it just now. You could, too. Damn it, you need me. I need you...."

The sound of the knock on the door startled them both. For a moment, neither of them moved but merely stood, staring at each other. All the answers to their questions hung achingly unspoken between them. Bewildered lovers turned strangers.

The pounding at the door continued and a muffled voice called out, "Dempsey? You in there?"

Mitch broke eye contact first. "The lab boys," he explained, his voice gruff with emotion as he turned away from her. "Cass," he said, stopping at the bedroom door and wheeling around to face her.

She looked at him, and he smiled a wry smile and held her again for just a moment with his eyes.

"Believe me, some things never change," he murmured.

Left alone, Cassie's body shook and her mind reeled as she sank back down onto the bed. She tried to resume the task that had brought her into the bedroom in the first place, but her heart wasn't in it. Her eyes were unseeing as she scooped up the remaining jewelry that lay scattered across the bed.

"Well, so much for the ozone layer," she muttered wearily and fell back against the pillows and closed her eyes. Run for your life, Chicken Little, the sky really is about to fall.

When she heard the sound of male voices in her living room, Cassie sat up and straightened her clothes. She had to recover her poise. The police would want her statement and an official account of anything missing.

Two uniformed policemen followed Mitch into the bedroom, and Cassie watched as they dusted the door and the furniture for fingerprints. When they finished in the bedroom, they moved into the kitchen. Cassie followed them, but soon, watching them move about her apartment with cool professional detachment, and listening to them discuss the possible scenarios of the break-in made her feel slightly sick to her stomach.

She needed to be alone, to continue her search, to think.

In the bathroom, she wet a washcloth and held it over her face until the nausea subsided. Grabbing a dry towel, she proceeded into her bedroom to wipe her furniture clean of the filmy layer left behind by the "lab boys."

After wiping down the nightstand, she opened the drawer and withdrew a framed picture, being careful to place it facedown on the bed. Neither she nor Mitch needed to see their engagement picture tonight.

Beneath a stack of letters and a box of stationery lay fifty dollars in cash. The folded stash her mother had always called "mad money" lay untouched at the bottom of the drawer.

"You may have interrupted him before he could grab anything of value," Mitch suggested from the doorway. His voice, she noticed with a twinge of resentment, was maddeningly steady and professional.

"Maybe," Cassie said quickly, replacing the picture and the money and closing the drawer. "Or maybe he just couldn't find what he was looking for. I did notice something else missing."

Mitch moved deeper into the room. "What?"

She ignored his question and reached for her purse. "Where are your friends?" she asked.

"They dusted the kitchen and the living room for prints and left. I told them I'd take your statement," he said. "Now will you please tell me what else is missing?"

"I'm not sure yet, but I think my neighbor's keys were taken."

"Your neighbor's keys?" Mitch asked, confusion etched in his expression.

"Yes. She's on vacation," Cassie said absently as she rummaged through her leather bag and finally dumped the contents onto the bed. "They're not here," she declared.

"Let's check the kitchen again," Mitch suggested.

Cassie brushed past him, concentrating on the grim conclusion that was quickly forming in her mind.

"They're gone," she announced after checking the empty peg and searching the kitchen and dining room again. "I know I left them hanging on the peg," Cassie insisted. "I remember hanging them there when I got back from feeding Caruso yesterday," she said as she moved back into the living room and grabbed her coat thrown over the back of the couch.

"Caruso?"

"Lucille's canary," Cassie murmured vaguely, shoving a hand into her coat pocket. "He stole those keys," she said softly as she pulled out of her pocket the keys they'd found at the scene of the hit and run. "But he made a mistake."

"What are you talking about, Cass?"

"He grabbed Lucille's keys, thinking he'd found what he was looking for. But don't you see, Mitch?" She turned her haunted gaze on him. "The burglar was looking for these."

Chapter Seven

The glowing digital numbers read six-thirty when Cassie slapped the buzzing alarm silent, groaned and promptly fell back to sleep. When next she awoke, it was with a start. *Nine forty-five!* With a groan, Cassie kicked off the covers and stumbled toward the shower.

Because she'd overslept, she be running to catch up all day, she told herself miserably. She rationalized that she'd had every reason to sleep in; it had been a pitifully short night. Mitch had waited until the locksmith had changed the locks before he'd left. And it had taken her best show of bravado to convince him to go.

Standing under the shower's stinging spray, Cassie groaned, remembering the warmth of his touch on her cheek, the desire she'd seen smoldering in his eyes—the same desperate desire she knew he'd seen reflecting back in her own. And finally, she remembered the emptiness that had engulfed her when he'd finally gone.

The familiar longing had stayed with her all night, preventing her from anything more than fitful sleep. With a look, a touch, a kiss he'd stirred life into the memories she'd tried so hard to still. Two long years erased in three short days.

Save yourself, Cassie, common sense warned as she ducked out of the shower and grabbed for a towel at the sound of the telephone ringing.

Hurrying across the bedroom, Cassie felt a quiver of anticipation as she reached for the phone, insanely hoping the voice she'd hear on the other end of the line would be Mitch's.

"Hello," she said breathlessly.

"Ms. Craig?" Arthur Lane's slightly nasal tone could never be mistaken for Mitch's mellow voice.

Swallowing her disappointment, Cassie forced a confident and professional tone. "Mr. Lane, this is Cassie. What can I do for you?"

"Ms. Craig, do you realize it's after ten? If it isn't too much trouble, would you be so kind as to tell me exactly when you're planning on coming to work today?"

His sarcasm put Cassie squarely on the defensive. "I don't believe anything in my contract requires me to punch a time clock, Arthur."

"We'll see about that, Ms. Craig," he countered. "In the meantime, I suggest you be in my office in thirty minutes."

Cassie bristled at his haughty and completely unauthorized command. "I'm afraid that won't be possible, Arthur," she said flatly. "I'm picking up supplies for the displays this morning and I hadn't planned on being downtown before noon." It was a bald-faced lie, but his attitude had pushed her to defiance.

"Ms. Craig, need I remind you that you are an employee of Hahn's department stores and, as such, under my direct supervision?"

As an independent contractor, the terms of her contract had been made with Grant Hahn, and Cassie felt a burning need to make that fact clear to the haughty store manager. "Correction," Cassie said indignantly, tightening her grip on the towel that had slipped sideways down her dripping torso. "*Grant Hahn* is my employer, Arthur. And if he has any problem with the hours I choose to work, I suggest you have him contact me."

Cassie was preparing to slam the receiver onto its cradle when she heard another voice come over the line.

"Ms. Craig?"

The voice that startled Cassie speechless belonged to none other than the man in question. Though most of her contact with her employer had been through Ruth Palmer, Cassie recognized Grant Hahn's deep, cultured voice immediately.

"Mr. Hahn?" The hollow sound echoing behind Cassie's words told her their conversation was being held over a speaker phone.

Cassie felt her stomach roll.

"I'm afraid something has happened to the displays, Ms. Craig. I need to speak to you as soon as possible," Grant explained. "Could you find a way to change your plans and get down to the store as soon as possible?"

"Of course, Mr. Hahn," she assured him, finding her voice at last.

"Thank you" came his curt reply.

Cassie stared at the phone a moment after she'd hung up, too startled at the moment to make much sense of the call.

When the phone rang again, Cassie snatched it up before the second ring. Arthur Lane's voice came over the line again. "Just wanted to let you know that Mr. Hahn and I will be waiting. Thirty minutes, Ms. Craig," he ordered. "Meet us in the display area."

A vivid picture of the store manager's victorious smirk made Cassie cringe. "Anything you say, Arthur," she said with exaggerated deference.

As she slipped into a green silk blouse and black denim pants, her anger at Arthur faded; something much more important occupied her thoughts. Grant Hahn had said something had happened to the displays. But what? A backdrop might have collapsed, or maybe they'd got word that something she'd ordered wouldn't be arriving in time.

No, Cassie told herself, something that simple wouldn't have prompted the attention of Grant Hahn, himself.

The phone rang again.

Damn it, Arthur! Cassie groaned inwardly as she rushed across the room and snatched up the receiver. How did the man expect her to get downtown in thirty minutes if he wouldn't leave her alone to get ready?

"Yes?" she snapped.

"And good morning to you, sunshine."

At the sound of Mitch's voice, Cassie's breath caught in her throat. Was she doomed to spend the whole day off balance?

"Mitch! I thought...that is, oh, never mind. I haven't got time to explain."

"I was just on my way over to see you, but it sounds as though you're in a hurry."

The disappointment Cassie heard in his voice produced a small wave of satisfaction inside her. "You're right. I should be leaving this second. There's been some kind of trouble at the store and I've got to get going." Cassie switched the phone to her other ear as she fumbled to slip her earrings in place. She'd have to look again tonight for those missing gold hoops, she reminded herself.

"Cassie, what is it?"

She heard and appreciated the concern in his voice. "I don't know. But I've got to go."

"I'll meet you."

"No, don't. Look, I can't talk right now. Call me later?" Why had she made it sound like an invitation?

"We'll meet tonight after you finish up at Hahn's. I need to get your statement about the break-in." He hesitated before adding, "And I think I may have some good news. I've identified the replica, Cass."

All thoughts of her meeting with Grant Hahn and Arthur Lane were instantly whisked away.

"You identified the charm? That's terrific, Mitch. But how?"

"I took the keys to a hobby shop. The owner found a model that matched our little token to a tee. It's a Rolls, Cass, a 1921 Rolls-Royce Silver Ghost. According to what I've been able to determine, it's an extremely rare and very valuable collector's item."

"Do you think we can find its owner? There can't be that many 1921 Silver Ghosts in Denver, can there?"

"I doubt it, but we'll soon find out. I plan to call in a couple of favors at Motor Vehicle the moment I hang up the phone. It could be a slow process of elimination, but we're close, Cass," Mitch promised. "This is the break we needed. In a few days' time, maybe less, we could know the identity of the hit-and-run victim."

"This is incredible," Cassie exclaimed. "Call me the moment you know anything," she insisted.

"The very moment," he promised brightly. "I'll see you later this evening."

On her way out of the bedroom, Cassie grabbed a bottle of cologne off the dresser and dropped it into her purse. The fact that she'd be seeing Mitch again that evening had nothing to do with her desire to feel feminine, she told herself firmly. But despite her best arguments, as she slammed out of her apartment and rushed down to the street, Cassie caught herself smiling.

FIFTEEN MINUTES LATER, Cassie pulled into the covered parking lot north of Hahn's. Snatching the keys from the ignition, she climbed out of the Honda and hurried down the alley behind the store.

Her attention was drawn to a police car as it passed by on the main street at the end of the alley. A disturbing mental image formed. It happened all the time. The sight of a black-and-white car evoked the image of Mitch, sexy and smiling. She felt the elevator drop in her stomach and a familiar tightening in her chest.

Just an old fantasy, Cassie's inner voice warned as she jammed her plastic security card into the electronic lockbox and tried to gather her wits for whatever awaited her inside.

A soft click told her the card had worked its magnetic magic, and in moments Cassie was winding her way through what seemed to be an unusually large crowd of customers on the main floor.

Up ahead, she caught sight of Grant Hahn and Arthur Lane locked in conversation as they walked side by side toward the displays. Cassie knew she'd be lying if she said she wasn't extremely nervous about facing Grant Hahn.

Aside from the fact that he was her boss, his impressive physical appearance, alone, was daunting. Tall and well built, he had the presence and bearing of an aristocrat. Though his long face was a bit too fine featured to be called classically handsome and his gray eyes were always cool and dispassionate, he did strike an impressive figure.

Cassie guessed every article of clothing he wore had been custom-made. From the expensive suit to the silk-blend dress shirt and designer tie, right down to the supple leather on his feet, everything that surrounded Grant Hahn spoke eloquently of his wealth and impeccable good taste.

In the times she'd come face-to-face with Grant, she couldn't remember ever seeing one of his prematurely silver hairs out of place. That was the scary part, Cassie decided. The real intimidation she felt whenever she came in contact with Grant Hahn stemmed from the aura of steely control he exuded.

She quickened her pace, but before she could catch up to the two men, they'd stepped up into the windows and disappeared behind the display's backdrop.

"Hey, kiddo, what's up?" Arlene asked.

"I have no idea," Cassie answered as she hurried past the last cosmetic counter. Was it her imagination or was Arlene's inquisitive gaze, along with the stares of nearly every other employee on the main floor, burning a hole through her back?

Drawing a steadying breath and pasting on a confident smile, Cassie stepped up into the window. Instantly her smile disappeared and that carefully drawn breath whooshed out of her as though an invisible fist had landed a blow to her solar plexus. She was barely aware of Grant and Arthur's presence as her startled eyes took in the terrible destruction that lay before her.

Garish splotches of red streaked the back wall. The swags of crimson velvet Cassie had so carefully draped along the back and sides of the display had been torn down and shredded. Cassie felt her stomach roll, the distinctive smell of wet paint overpowering and nauseating.

Walking numbly toward the center of the display, she heard glass crunch under her feet. Looking down, she recognized the shattered remains of the two large lamps she'd positioned to highlight the display. Her hands flew up to her mouth to stifle a gasp when she spotted the line of wooden soldiers she'd arranged just last night. Even now the brightly colored regiment was standing at perfect attention just as she'd left them, but with one terrible exception, each and every one had been systematically beheaded.

Cassie's vision blurred as startled tears nipped her eyes, the reality of the moment, the cold, stark, malicious reality nearly overwhelming her.

"My God," she whispered. "What happened?"

"*That* is the question exactly," Arthur declared, his eyebrows raised suspiciously. "The displays were found this way when the store was opened this morning."

"Have you called the police?" Cassie asked numbly.

"There's no need for that," Grant put in quickly. "I'm sure this is something that can be resolved in-house."

"But this vandalism should be reported. The police should be called," Cassie persisted, confused by Grant's blasé attitude.

"Ms. Craig," Arthur Lane interrupted, "Hahn's department stores have the finest state-of-the-art security system available. I assure you we would know if there'd been a break-in," he stated emphatically, the small red carnation in his lapel bobbing as his puny chest expanded.

"Then how do you explain all this?" Cassie asked.

"We'll find the explanation, Ms. Craig," Grant reassured her, his voice steady and confident.

"Now, why don't you just tell us what went on here last night, Ms. Craig, and save us all a lot of trouble?" Arthur suggested.

Cassie stood staring at him, unblinking and speechless as the shock of his accusation jolted through her.

"Exactly what time did you leave the store last night?"

"What? I-I don't know. It was late, around eight or eight-thirty, I guess," she stammered.

"Never mind. We'll have a record on the electronic lock system of the exact time you left," Arthur said impatiently. "I have no doubt that between the time you left last night and the time the store was opened this morning, no one else was on the premises."

Cassie blinked disbelieving. Arthur's absurd implication that she'd had something to do with the destruction of the displays finally seeped through her numbed senses.

"Just what are you getting at?" she demanded, her voice not sounding nearly as steady as she would have liked.

"What I'm getting at, Ms. Craig, is that you were the last one in the displays last night."

Cassie glared at him, still disbelieving. His accusations were too ridiculous to be taken seriously.

"But why in heaven's name would I do such a thing?" she demanded.

"I'm sure I wouldn't know," Arthur said flippantly. "Some people just crave attention, I guess. You artsy types more than others."

"That's insane!" Cassie snapped. "What could I possibly hope to gain by destroying my own work?"

"A chance for a little more publicity, maybe?" Arthur suggested, his thin lips curved into a smirk.

Outraged, Cassie swung her attention to Grant Hahn for support, but his face was a rigid and emotionless mask.

Had the whole world gone mad? "Surely, Mr. Hahn, *you* don't think I had anything to do with this—this mess?"

With a quick wave of his manicured hand, Grant dismissed Cassie's question and any further accusations that might be leveled by Arthur.

"Ms. Craig, I don't know what I think at this point. Arthur, we'll discuss this further in my office."

Discuss what? Cassie's mind screamed. Instead of standing around listening to Arthur Lane's ridiculous accusations, they should be calling the police. The whole world really had gone crazy. Why had she even bothered to crawl out of bed this morning?

"In the meantime," Grant continued, "The custodians have hung a drape over the windows until the displays can be cleaned up. We didn't want any more of our customers getting a look at this mess. The workers should arrive any moment. You'll remain to supervise their work, Ms. Craig?"

"Of course," Cassie said, nodding solemnly.

He gave her a curt nod of dismissal and took a last disgusted look at the devastation that surrounded him.

"I'll be in my office all afternoon. Would you please stop by on your way out."

Again Cassie nodded, her mind reeling. What did he mean, "on her way out"? Did he mean "on your way home" or "on your way to the unemployment line"? Cassie wondered miserably as she watched her employer move across the displays, the sound of glass crunching beneath his expensive Italian shoes. Arthur Lane followed, despite the glare Cassie leveled at him that should have turned him to stone.

As soon as the two men left, Cassie gave way to her emotions and slumped down onto the floor despondently. For a moment she could only sit and stare, still not quite believing the vicious destruction even though she saw it with her own eyes.

After a moment she drew her legs up in front of her, clasped her arms around them and rested her chin on her knees. Squeezing her eyes closed, she fought the bitter tears that threatened to fall.

Why would Arthur suspect she'd had anything to do with this? she wondered again. And what if Grant Hahn shared his manager's opinion and decided she was some kind neurotic artist with a passion for publicity? At the end of this day would she still have a contract with Hahn's? A future in Denver as a designer?

A shuffling noise behind her interrupted her grim introspection. She glanced over to see Mitch stepping up into the window. His shocked stare ricocheted from the ruined display to Cassie's face.

"What the hell . . . ?"

"That seems to be the question of the day," Cassie muttered, rising to stand beside him and scrambling to recover the poise she'd felt crumbling from the moment she'd awakened this morning.

In a rush of words she explained the phone call from Arthur Lane and the ridiculous accusations that had greeted her when she arrived at Hahn's and was confronted by Grant Hahn and his detestable store manager.

As Mitch listened, his dark brows drew together in a grim frown. "What did the police say?"

"They were never called." The absurdity still choked her.

"What? Why not?"

"Who knows?" Cassie shrugged. "It seems Grant Hahn has built an impenetrable, self-contained little kingdom here. He makes it very clear he doesn't want the press, the police or anyone else from the outside interfering."

Mitch shook his head. "Sounds suspicious to me."

"Arthur Lane said the displays were found in this condition when the store was opened. I can't believe they suspect I had something to do with all of this." Her voice cracked.

"It's a nightmare, Mitch," she whispered. "First the hit and run, the break-in last night... and now this!"

Her eyes shimmered as she stared up at him, asking questions for which he had no answers.

"Did they actually accuse you?" he asked, his hand coming to rest reassuringly on her arm.

"Not in so many words, but Arthur's implication was clear. He seems to have some insane notion that I crave publicity." She sighed, swallowing her despair.

Scuffing sounds behind them cut off Mitch's reply and announced the arrival of two uniformed custodians.

Cassie watched Mitch help set up one of the steel ladders the two men had brought with them. He climbed to the top and proceeded to assist the custodians with the heavy black drapes. She watched his confident and self-assured movement, and for the second time in the past twenty-four hours she felt strengthened by his presence.

As the three men hung the drapes, Cassie began the arduous task of cleanup. A quick assessment told her the displays were very nearly a total loss. Even if

Hahn's insurance covered vandalism, Cassie wondered how she'd ever find the time to replace all the supplies she'd lost and finish the windows by the December first deadline outlined in her contract. It just couldn't be done, she told herself despondently.

A sudden mental picture of Arthur Lane's self-satisfied smirk sparked the anger and indignation Cassie needed to face the overwhelming task of rebuilding the displays. With that firm mental shake, Cassie began to draw a mental outline of the task before her, resolving to not only do whatever she had to do to meet her deadline, but to make the holiday windows a stunning success, as well. Immediately she began to feel better.

Twenty minutes later, the entire length of the windows across the front of the store was shrouded in black, and the paint-spattered and ruined velvet swags had been stuffed into large black garbage bags.

Cassie examined one of the headless wooden soldiers and decided that with a little glue and patience they could be repaired.

"Need anything else?" asked the taller custodian, whose name—Bill—was stitched in gold on his uniform pocket.

"I think that will about do it." Cassie sighed as she finished sweeping up the last of the slivered glass.

"Thanks, guys." She offered them a grateful smile.

"Sure thing," Bill said, his expression sympathetic.

"It's a darn shame what happened here." The other custodian, whose name was obliterated by a smudge of grease, added. As he folded up the ladder and leaned it against the back wall, he said, "The windows were looking real pretty, too."

"Thanks," Cassie said again.

"Did either of you notice anything unusual last night or this morning? Anyone hanging around the displays or tampering with the windows?" Mitch asked. Cassie noticed his cop voice was firmly in place this morning.

The two men shook their heads. "Not that I can remember," Bill said. "But then again. I was off last night and to tell you the truth," he confided, "I was running kinda late this morning. Got a new baby," he informed them, his chest swelling and his face beaming with pride. "And let me tell you, that boy's got himself a set of lungs! Kept me and the wife up almost all night. That's why I overslept, I guess."

The second custodian shook his head and chuckled. "Old Arthur was really P.O.ed."

"Really?" Mitch prodded.

Bill scowled. "I wasn't more than ten or fifteen minutes late, but he had to open up. First time in five years I've been late to work and he reads me the riot act."

Cassie could understand Bill's resentment of Arthur Lane's unfair treatment of his subordinates.

"Tells me he'll cover for me," Bill explained. "Lucky me, indebted to that snake!"

The empathy Cassie felt for her fellow employee and the anger she felt toward Arthur Lane was edged away by a vague suspicion nagging at the back of her mind. Something just didn't ring true. So far as she'd been able to tell, Arthur Lane wouldn't put himself out for anyone. Though she couldn't prove it, yet, Cassie felt instinctively that Arthur's uncharacteristically benevolent behavior toward Bill had something to do with the vandalism.

"Anyway, it's a darn shame about your windows, miss. We know you've been working real hard every night." Bill's comments pulled Cassie's attention back to the conversation.

She nodded her thanks. "Hopefully in a few days I'll have it looking even better than before."

"That's the way," Bill put in enthusiastically and then nodding to his assistant, left Cassie and Mitch alone once more.

"Feeling better?" Mitch asked.

Cassie smiled for his sake. "With some extra evening hours and a little creativity in procuring replacement supplies, I think I can still make my deadline. Now all I have to do is survive my meeting with Grant Hahn."

"You'll do just fine," Mitch assured her.

"Why do you suppose Arthur lied to me, Mitch?"

"About what?"

"Well, maybe it wasn't exactly a lie, but it was certainly an evasion of the exact truth. I think he deliberately led me to believe that someone else opened the store this morning. And I'll bet he hoped Grant Hahn believed the same thing."

"But why would he do that?" Mitch asked, his expression thoughtful.

"I'm not sure unless he had something to do with the vandalism. That would explain his strange offer to cover for Bill being late. Arthur Lane isn't the type to do a favor for anyone unless it benefits him directly or he thinks he could exact a payback later."

"Or maybe to cover his own hide?"

Cassie nodded.

"It sounds like something we should look into," Mitch said.

"Oh! I'd completely forgotten about the replica," Cassie exclaimed. "Is that why you're here? You found the owner?"

Mitch shook his head. "Not yet. I'm afraid these things take time, Cass."

She swallowed her disappointment with a sigh. "Well, right now time is something I'm out of. As soon as I pack these away, I'd better get up to Grant Hahn's office." Mitch helped her quickly pile the mutilated wooden soldiers into a cardboard box.

"I'll take these guys home and perform reconstructive surgery tonight," Cassie said with a grim smile.

"Could you use some assistance in the O.R., Dr. Craig?"

Common sense told her to turn him down, but once again, where Mitch Dempsey was concerned, her heart overruled her head. "Sure," she said quickly.

"Great. I'll pick up dinner at Jade Gardens and drop by around seven. Kung Pao beef and wontons, right?"

Cassie nodded, feeling warmed and somehow comforted by his having remembered. Would he remember the side order of fried rice and the plum wine, as well, she wondered.

They reached for the last soldier at the same time. Mitch's hand covered hers and a burst of tenderness erupted inside her. She pulled her hand away reluctantly and avoided his gaze by averting her own to the wooden soldier in her hand.

"What's this?" she asked, noticing for the first time the small piece of white paper tucked under the soldier's rigid arm. Quickly she unfolded the small note. Her breath caught as she read the message scrawled in black.

Feeling the blood drain from her face, Cassie reached for the steadying force of Mitch's right arm.

"Cassie, what is it? What's wrong?" he asked seizing the paper from her trembling hands.

A dark scowl moved across his face like the shadow of an angry thundercloud.

"'Forget what you saw,'" Mitch read aloud. "What the hell is this?"

"We both know who wrote it," she replied hoarsely, searching his face for the contradiction she hoped would be forthcoming.

But Mitch's silence shouted his agreement. The truth sent a rush of rage coursing through her, and a shiver of dread racing up her spine.

The driver. He knew Cassie's identity and he knew she had witnessed his crime, and he meant to stop her from coming forth with the truth. He'd broken into her apartment. He'd vandalized the displays. And the threatening note was his next deadly move.

Chapter Eight

Arthur moved across the outer office and closed the door behind him before approaching his employer's gleaming mahogany desk.

"You're a fool, Arthur," Grant Hahn said matter-of-factly. "A damn fool."

"She could have done it." Arthur protested. "She's out for all the publicity she can get. Agreeing to be interviewed by that reporter proves it."

"But her name didn't even appear in that article, Arthur. What kind of publicity could she have hoped to gain?" Grant's voice was even and unemotional.

"Who can say what she was thinking? You saw for yourself how she is, emotional, unstable. She spoke to that reporter and she was just dying to get the police involved, today. And the *Herald*, too, no doubt."

Grant shook his head. "Go back to work, Arthur," he ordered. "I'll think about what you've said."

Arthur hesitated at the door.

"What are you waiting for?" Grant asked impatiently. "Surely there must be someone you haven't yet bullied this morning."

Arthur tipped his chin indignantly. "I don't deserve that, Mr. Hahn." He sniffed. "I do the best I can. It's not an easy task dealing with all these different personalities. I've made a study of human nature, you know, and I take great pride in my abilities."

"Right," Grant muttered without looking up as Arthur reached for the door. Grant pressed the intercom button on his phone, which allowed him to talk to his outer office.

"Ruth, bring me the security print-out for the past twenty-four hours."

Arthur's hand froze on the doorknob and he whirled around to face his employer.

"Let me run that for you, Mr. Hahn. You know how nervous Ruth is around the new security system. The last time she tinkered with it, we had to call in a team of the security company's service people and they spent half a day getting things straightened out. Her mistake cost us a pretty penny. Our service contract doesn't cover inept secretaries, you know."

Grant studied his store manager for a moment. Arthur did always seem to have the best interests of the company in mind. Maybe that's why Grant put up with him, despite his personal dislike for the man and his condescending ways.

"All right, Arthur. Tell Ruth on your way out that you'll be running the report. Get that summary to me by this afternoon. If it shows that anyone checked through the system between the time Ms. Craig left and our custodian opened this morning, I want to know."

"Certainly," Arthur agreed.

His officious assistant manager probably was the right person to audit the security report, Grant told himself after Arthur left the office. If any of the several employees who'd been issued security cards had returned to Hahn's last night after Cassie Craig had left, Arthur Lane would be just the man to report them.

CASSIE TOOK A DEEP BREATH before she opened the door to the executive offices and stepped in. She was greeted by Ruth Palmer's steady smile.

"Hello, Ruth," Cassie said.

"Cassie." Ruth acknowledged her with a curt nod.

"He's expecting you," Ruth said, glancing over her shoulder at the wide oak door behind her. "I'll tell him you're here." Ruth picked up the phone, touched a button and announced Cassie's arrival.

"Go on in," Ruth said pleasantly.

Cassie took a deep breath and opened the door and walked briskly across the well-appointed office. Grant stood up behind his desk to greet her. "Ms. Craig," he said, "won't you sit down?"

Ignoring his offer, Cassie launched into the words that had been burning a hole through her mind ever since Arthur Lane had leveled his accusations at her.

"I can't work where I'm not trusted, Mr. Hahn," she informed him, moving up to his desk and standing rigidly in front of it.

Her fingers closed around the note in her pocket. If she pulled it out now and showed it to him, proving she'd had nothing to do with the destruction of the displays, she'd always wonder if he'd shared Arthur's view of her guilt. At this point, retaining her job seemed a distant second to the principle involved.

"Please sit down, Ms. Craig," he said with a cool smile, motioning to one of the four leather chairs arranged in a semicircle in front of his desk.

Cassie eased reluctantly onto the edge of the chair nearest her.

"How's the cleanup going?" he asked.

"It's finished," she replied quickly.

"Good. Now, I think our main objective ought to be getting the displays back on schedule, don't you? Purchase whatever you need to replace the ruined materials and hire an assistant if you think it's necessary."

Stunned, Cassie could only stare at him, half-afraid to believe she'd heard him correctly. After this morning's encounter, she'd expected her walking papers to be waiting for her. But things seemed to have changed, and Grant Hahn was behaving like the rational, reasonable businessman she'd always assumed him to be.

"You mean you still want me to do the holiday windows?"

Grant stared at her, unblinking. "Of course. Why wouldn't I?"

"B-but Arthur, that is, Mr. Lane accused me of malicious vandalism." Her voice rose.

"Never mind Arthur," Grant said easily. "Now, do you think you'll be able to meet the December first deadline or not?"

Cassie nodded. "Yes, I will," she assured him.

"Good." He said. His tone and body language told Cassie that as far as he was concerned, their meeting had come to a close.

But the myriad of questions swirling around in Cassie's mind still needed answers. She shifted uneasily in the chair, uncertain how and where to begin.

"Something else, Ms. Craig?" he asked, dragging his attention away from the stack of papers into which he seemed in the past few moments to have become suddenly and completely absorbed.

"Well, yes, there is more." Cassie spoke quickly before she lost the courage to confront him. "There's the matter of the vandalism, Mr. Hahn. I still don't understand why the police weren't called. What if something like this happens again? Next time the damage could be irreparable. Someone could get hurt. We can't afford to just ignore what happened."

"We haven't ignored anything, Ms. Craig," he replied coolly.

Cassie felt the blood rising to her cheeks. "Then what are you going to do to find the person responsible?" she demanded.

"As Arthur pointed out to you earlier," he explained impatiently, "Hahn's has one of the finest security systems in the business. If the damage to the displays was deliberate, as you seem determined to believe, we'll know soon enough."

"But you don't believe it was deliberate, do you?" Cassie challenged, surprised and disturbed by this newest development. "You saw with your own eyes the damage, the destruction..."

"I never jump to conclusions, Ms. Craig. Accidents happen. A gallon of red paint can make quite a mess when it's spilled."

Cassie jumped to her feet, snatched the anonymous note from her pocket and thrust it across the desk at him. "That paint was not accidentally spilled and this proves it. Was this note written by accident?"

Cassie glared at him as he gave the note a cursory glance and handed it back to her. "What is this supposed to mean? I don't have time for riddles, Ms. Craig."

"What this means, Mr. Hahn, is that someone's threatening me. The hit and run . . ."

"So we're back to that, now?" His steely indifference was maddening.

"Yes," she said levelly, tamping down her outrage at his attitude. "I believe the hit and run I witnessed Sunday night is the basis for all of this. The note, the vandalism of the displays. Did you know my apartment was burglarized last night?"

"And what do the police say about this supposed hit and run of yours, Ms. Craig?" His steady gaze never wavered.

Cassie only shook her head.

"The police were called, weren't they?" he prodded.

"You know very well the police were called," Cassie said, despising the gleam of victory she saw reflected in his cold gray eyes. "What else could I have done?"

"And what did the police come up with?" he asked with feigned innocence.

"We both know the outcome of the police investigation," she said quietly. "But the police were mistaken."

"We're all wrong. Isn't that right, Ms. Craig? The Denver Police Department, Mr. Lane, me. We're all working together in some sort of bizarre collusion to prevent you from completing the displays on time."

"Don't be ridiculous," she snapped.

"Ridiculous, indeed," Grant agreed, his tone sickeningly patronizing. "Take my advice, Ms. Craig, finish the job you've been contracted to do. Leave the security of Hahn's to me and that of the city of Denver to the police."

Cassie's indignation reached the boiling point as Grant rose and moved toward the door.

"If you feel you're able to complete the project you've agreed to do for us, I'm willing to work with you. If not..." He spread his arms out in a helpless gesture. "Now, if you'll excuse me, I have a very busy day scheduled."

Cassie knew when she had hit a brick wall. The way he'd presented the situation, with all the facts misconstrued and twisted, she'd never had a chance of reaching him. He'd made it clear that anything or anyone who represented even a vague threat to the image of Hahn's department stores would be dismissed or discredited.

Cassie glanced over her shoulder at the elaborate builder's model as she headed for the door. So much for her chance of landing the Hahn account for the Crystal Creek store's windows. At this rate, she'd be lucky to get the contract to decorate the Hahn family doghouse. She had little left to lose.

With that last bitter realization, she launched one final appeal to reason. "All I'm *interested* in, Mr.

Hahn," she said, trying to contain her anger as he moved with her toward the door, "is making sure that nothing like this happens again."

"Then we share a common interest," he said solicitously as he opened the door and ushered her out. "Ruth will give you the purchase order numbers for the larger items and just make a list of any out-of-pocket expenses you might incur in repairing the display. Ruth will see to it that you're reimbursed."

But can't you see this isn't about reimbursements or purchase orders? Cassie wanted to shout and she opened her mouth to tell him just that, but before she had the chance to say another word, he stepped inside his office and closed the door in her face.

"Good day, Ms. Craig," Ruth Palmer said as she reached for the ringing telephone.

Cassie stalked from the outer office and into the hallway, her frustration and anger nearly blinding her as she hurried toward the elevator. She really should go back to the displays and inventory the supplies she needed to finish the job, she told herself. But it would have to wait. At this moment, with her credibility and her career teetering precariously on the edge of ruin, all she wanted to do was to run as far away from Hahn's as possible.

A SKITTERING SOUND CAME from the bird cage sitting above her on the kitchen counter. Though the building super had refused to give Cassie the spare key to 306, he did agree to let her in tonight long enough to move Caruso into her own apartment.

"Be with you in a minute, little guy," Cassie promised. Caruso was pacing his cage, letting her know it was past his bedtime. Lucille must keep her small orange friend on a tight schedule, Cassie mused as she draped the brightly embroidered scarf over the cage.

The antique school clock hanging above the dining room table chimed nine. "Two hours late and not so much as a phone call. Way to go, Dempsey," she muttered, dropping down onto the newspapers that covered the kitchen floor. This day was a bust from start to finish, Cassie told herself miserably.

Open cans of paint and glue surrounded her. The cold remains of a take-out pizza sat in its soggy box beside her.

"Didn't I tell you not to believe him, Sam? Didn't I warn you?" Cassie asked the mannequin whose arms were raised at a curious angle to accommodate the clothesline Cassie had stretched the length of the apartment. The other end of the long thin cord was attached to the coat tree beside the front door.

All along the line hung a score of freshly painted sugarplum fairies, their dreamlike fairy qualities duly restored. Each one wore a fluffy new tutu of pastel netting and a bright smile courtesy of Cassie's careful hand and a jar of pink paint.

Stretching her arms out behind her, Cassie leaned back and admired her handiwork with grim satisfaction. If only there was a way to repair her own tattered holiday dreams as easily.

A sharp knock at her door made Cassie jump to her feet. Halfway across the room, she stopped. "Dempsey," she mumbled. "Don't you dare let him in, Sam."

A series of quick impatient taps was followed by the sound of his voice. "Cassie? Are you in there? It's Mitch."

"Go away," Cassie yelled. "You have the wrong apartment. No one here called the police."

"Cassie, open up," Mitch said in his patented cop voice. "I've got something to show you."

Cassie shook her head. "Forget it, Dempsey. I've already seen everything you've got to show and I'm not interested anymore."

"Damn it, Cass," she heard him mutter. "This is important. I'm not playing games. Now let me in."

Moving woodenly toward the door, she leaned against it and closed her eyes. "Get a warrant, Officer," she said with forced bravado. If she was smart, Cassie warned herself as she felt her resolve crumbling, even a court order signed by a supreme court justice wouldn't let Mitch Dempsey back into her life.

A scraping sound accompanied the envelope she saw being shoved under her door from the outside. Giving in to her natural curiosity, she reached down and picked it up. It wasn't sealed. Lifting the flap, Cassie peered inside.

"My earrings!" she exclaimed, her hand on the doorknob. "You found them. Dempsey, you caught my burglar!"

Chapter Nine

"Are you sure those are your earrings? Absolutely sure?" Mitch asked, his expression deadly serious.

"Why, yes. I think so," Cassie said as she stared down at the small gold hoops in her palm, studying them more closely. "Yes, they're mine. I'm sure. What is it, Mitch? What's wrong?"

Mitch took her arm and maneuvered them both into the living room, pushing the door closed behind them.

"I think they've found the body of your hit-and-run victim, Cass," he said gently, his gaze locked on her face.

"Oh, my God," Cassie gasped, sinking down onto the sofa. "The body. Then he's dead," she said in a half whisper. "I'd so hoped..."

Mitch sat down beside her and put his arms around her. "I know. So did I."

For a long moment, Cassie huddled in the protective circle of his arms, not caring whether it was right or wrong to be there.

"Where, Mitch? Where... and how did they find him?" Cassie's voice was shaky as she drew slowly out of his embrace.

As Mitch explained, Cassie felt alternately shocked and confused. According to Mitch, the sheriff's department had responded early Sunday morning to a report of a vehicle having careened off a narrow mountain road west of Denver.

"When the emergency units arrived, they found the burned-out hulk of a demolished pickup truck. Inside were the barest remains of a human being," Mitch said, his eyes studying her carefully for the impact of his words.

Cassie shuddered and wrapped her arms around herself.

"What happened? Do they know?"

"There's a rowdy bar not too far from the site where the pickup left the road. The theory that the sheriff's department has adopted is that the driver got juiced up at the bar and couldn't make the curve. They're saying the pickup caught fire as it crashed and rolled down the mountainside."

"How awful." Cassie shuddered. "But wait a minute, what's this got to do with the hit and run in downtown Denver? Did I miss something?"

He reached over and touched the earrings she still held in the palm of her hand. "Your earrings were found near the scene of the wreckage, Cass."

"What?" Cassie exclaimed. "Wait a minute. Back up. How did you find out about the accident, Mitch? That mountain area is well outside the jurisdiction of the Denver PD, isn't it?"

Mitch nodded. "When you're a second-generation cop in this town you get to know a lot of people in the field. Anyway, Monday morning I spread the word that

I wanted to be informed of any unusual incidents or serious injuries that were reported in or around the Denver area either late Sunday night or early Monday morning. When a friend from the Jefferson County Sheriff's Department called and told me about the accident, I drove out this afternoon to take a look."

"And that's why you forgot all about dinner," Cassie added.

"Damn!" Mitch smacked his forehead with his palm. "No wonder you wouldn't let me in. I'm sorry, babe."

She waved her hand, dismissing his apology and fighting to ignore the term of endearment she hadn't heard in two years. "Forget it. It doesn't matter. Go on. I'm still thoroughly confused. Tell me the rest."

"Well, by the time I drove out to the sheriff's office, I'd just about convinced myself I was wasting my time. But when my friend showed me the evidence gathered at the scene and I saw these—" he frowned and picked up the gold hoops "—I remembered you said you'd lost a pair of earrings and I thought we just might have something."

"So the man killed in the accident was my burglar?" Cassie asked, still confused.

"The accident took place Sunday night, Cass. Your apartment was burglarized on Tuesday."

"Right." Cassie frowned as she tried to piece it all together.

"Anyway, while I was still there, they identified the accident victim by tracing the serial number of the pickup." Cassie listened intently as Mitch told her the dead man's name was Cal Vantana and explained that

Vantana had a record that read like a freshman class in criminology.

"Petty theft, aggravated assault, illegal gaming, possession of stolen goods. Nothing really serious, but hardly a solid citizen, either. He'd been paroled from the state pen only a couple of months ago."

Mitch stopped talking and stared at her.

"Go on, Mitch. Tell me the rest."

"I've got a copy of his mug shots, Cass. I want you to take a look if you think you're up to it."

Cassie nodded tentatively. "Well, sure, I'll take a look. But I still don't see what any of this has to do with the hit and run."

Mitch pulled the grainy black-and-white photos from his jacket pocket and handed them to her.

"My God," Cassie whispered as she stared at the pictures she held in her trembling hands. "It's him! The man I saw run down in front of Hahn's. It's him!"

Mitch laid the pictures down on the coffee table and took her hand. "The earrings were found in the pocket of a bloodstained jacket found near the scene," he said softly.

Cassie gasped and her hands flew up to her mouth. "I remember now, Mitch! Earlier that night I took my earrings off and stuffed them into my pocket. I put my jacket over him, Mitch. I tried to cover him. He was so cold." Her voice trailed away.

She sat staring, and the haunted look in her shimmering green eyes told him she was reliving the terrible scene.

"You know what this means, don't you?" she said, her voice brittle.

Mitch nodded as he took her hand. "You witnessed a murder, Cassie. A cold-blooded murder."

"BUT SHE ID'D HIM, Andy," Mitch insisted. "She recognized Vantana as the man she saw run down outside of Hahn's."

The heavyset, thick-necked detective studied Mitch with tired brown eyes. He let a rush of cigarette smoke escape with his impatient sigh and ran his stubby fingers through his thinning gray hair. A battered nameplate that read Captain Andrew P. Anderson sat precariously close to the edge of the cluttered desk.

"You believe her?" Anderson asked, one bushy salt-and-pepper eyebrow raised cynically.

"I do," Mitch said flatly.

As Anderson took another long drag from his cigarette, pieces of ash tumbled unnoticed down his shirt-front.

"The question is, do you believe her because you're a good cop or because you're still in love with her?"

Mitch was on his feet. "Oh, to hell with you, Andy. Give me a break! We go back too far for that kind of crap."

"Damn it, Dempsey, you give *me* a friggin' break. Listen to the facts one damn minute, will you? The lady calls us to the scene of a crime, but there's no crime. Then her apartment is robbed, but nothing's missing and there's no sign of forced entry, no prints.

"Now you tell me the body found at the bottom of Lookout Mountain in Jefferson County is the same guy your girlfriend saw splattered on the pavement four days ago."

"The body could have been moved," Mitch suggested.

"Or it could have been a drunk she saw stretched out on the street the way Officer Sommerfield explained in his report."

"A man is dead," Mitch pointed out.

"Right," Anderson agreed. "And the coroner's report rules the cause of death accidental. It says Vantana died of 'multiple and serious injuries sustained in the crash and ensuing fire.' Case closed."

Mitch shook his head. "Come on, Andy, you know as well as I do that's the explanation the medical examiners use when there's nothing left to autopsy."

"Do I?" Anderson challenged, the veins on his forehead bulging. "Well, I'll tell you something else I know, Dempsey, you're way out of line on this thing. You've lost your objectivity. Besides, you're supposed to be on vacation. Remember?"

Mitch ignored Anderson's last remarks. "Open the case back up, Andy. Give it to me. I'll work on it on my own time."

"Can't do it," Anderson said flatly.

"Can't or won't?" Mitch growled.

"Look, you're a good cop, Dempsey, just like your old man. You're a good friend, too," the older cop added gruffly. "And that's why I'm trying to help you. You're making this thing personal."

Mitch said nothing but continued to level Anderson with a steely glare. A moment of strained silence passed between them.

"Oh, what the hell. Go ahead," Anderson grumbled. "Look around. Satisfy yourself. Ten bucks says that pile of ash and bone sitting in the lab will only tell you things are exactly what they appear to be—accidental death, Mitch—nothing more, nothing less.''

"I'll take that bet," Mitch said quickly.

Anderson's frown deepened, his fleshy forehead folding into creases like someone's pet basset hound. "But don't let me see it. Understand? If I so much as get a whiff of you breaking or even bending the rules, I'll bust your butt six ways to Sunday. That's a promise.''

Mitch allowed himself a small smile. "Thanks, Andy.''

"Believe me, I'm not doing you any favors. I've seen cops go through this before. Chasing after an obsession. It eats them alive. You'd better be sure she's worth it, Dempsey. Damn sure," Anderson warned.

"She is, Chief," Mitch said as he reached for the door. "Believe me, she is.''

Chief Anderson's words followed Mitch out of the office. His boss had issued a clear warning. Mitch knew he'd have to tread lightly, using his resources and favors sparingly and discreetly. But if it came down to needing more than he could get officially, then what? Would he use his connections, his friends in and out of the department, anything and everything at his disposal to prove Cassie right? If it came right down to it, what wouldn't he do for her?

Searching for the answers to his questions left him feeling deeply disturbed and distracted, two emotions he knew a cop couldn't afford to feel if he wanted to stay a cop. If he wanted to stay alive.

LATER THAT AFTERNOON when Mitch told Cassie he'd discovered Cal Vantana had had a roommate and that he was planning on talking to the man, she'd insisted he take her along for the interview. Though Mitch had known it would be a waste of his energy, he tried to argue her out of it anyway.

"It's my life that's been threatened, Mitch," she'd declared flatly. "If anyone has a right to ask questions, I do. And besides," she'd argued, "I want to see what his life was like, how and where he lived."

Mitch had a pretty good idea what ex-convict Cal Vantana's life had been like. His arrest record said it all. But he understood Cassie's need to know more, so in the end, he'd relented. Besides, his knowledge of his ex-fiancée's modus operandi told him it would do him no good to refuse. Cassie was a very determined woman. He knew darned well if he'd turned her down, she'd have pursued her investigation with or without him. At least if she was with him, he could protect her, not only from the driver, but from her own stubborn though well-intentioned impulses.

Mitch signaled to turn off Sixth Avenue and glanced over at Cassie. In her baggy cable-knit sweater and faded jeans she looked small and vulnerable. But to him, no matter what she wore, she was the most beautiful woman in the world. Her enthusiasm for life, her compassion and caring, the radiance of the inner Cassie shone with a special brightness that took his breath away.

"What street are we looking for?" she asked, pulling him out of his thoughts.

"Carr. It should be the next through street."

Mitch made a left and drove slowly down the quiet tree-lined street searching for the right house number.

"There it is," he murmured. "Ten-sixty." He pulled the Porsche up to the curb and parked in front of a small white clapboard house on the corner.

So this is where Cal Vantana lived, Cassie thought. She didn't know exactly what she'd pictured as his place of residence, but the quiet suburban street just didn't fit the image of an ex-con who'd died a violent and mysterious death.

"According to his parole officer, Cal moved in less than a month ago. His roommate has lived here only a little longer," Mitch informed her.

He got out and came around to open the door for Cassie, but she was already out of the car and waiting for him on the sidewalk.

Though she'd insisted on coming along, all of the sudden questioning Cal's roommate didn't seem right to her somehow. It seemed improper, insensitive. In all probability the men had been friends. Cal Vantana's remains hadn't even been properly interred.

"Is Cal's roommate an ex-con?" Cassie asked as they headed for the front door.

"No. Jordan Sloane is as clean as the driven snow, not even so much as a parking ticket." The only shred of incriminating evidence Mitch had on Sloane was the statement of a neighbor who said she saw him driving Cal's pickup early on Sunday. It wasn't much.

Mitch rang the bell and in a moment Cassie heard a rustling sound on the other side of the door.

A tall, extremely good-looking young man dressed in dark slacks and a crisp white shirt opened the door.

Something about his blue eyes looked a bit unnatural, a little too blue. Colored contacts, Cassie decided as she watched his eyes flick intelligently between her and Mitch, coming to rest finally on her.

"Jordan Sloane?" Mitch asked.

"Yes," the young man replied, his interest and his friendly smile firmly locked on Cassie. Along with Jordan Sloane's startling, almost-too-perfect looks, they were greeted by the strong, slightly sickening smell of an artificial fragrance coming from inside the house. Cassie figured Sloane must have sprayed the room with an air freshener moments before he'd opened the door. Despite the cloying smell of the aerosol spray, Cassie caught the distinct odor of a cat box and stale cigarette smoke.

Mitch flipped open a small leather badge case. "Detective Dempsey, Denver police. I phoned earlier?"

The badge snapped Sloane's attention off Cassie and onto the business at hand.

"Of course," he said nervously. "I remember."

"And this is Cassandra Craig," Mitch said without blinking as he took her hand and stepped across the threshold. "May we come in?"

Cassie bristled at his possessive gesture. She wanted to say something, scald him with some scathing remark, but she checked the impulse, realizing how stupid they'd look standing in Jordan Sloane's doorway, arguing.

Instead she dug her nails into his palms and smiled at him sweetly, batting her lashes innocently when he flinched.

"You've come about Cal," Jordan Sloane said, apparently unaware of the private drama being played out between them.

"Yes. We were hoping you could shed some light on the circumstances surrounding his death," Mitch replied, following as Sloane led them into the sparsely furnished but well-kept living room.

Cassie felt Jordan Sloane's too-blue eyes still on her as he offered them a seat on a worn love seat positioned next to a fireplace that covered the north wall of the small room. As Mitch sat down, he shoved his badge case back into his pocket. As he did, a set of keys clattered to the floor.

Cassie saw immediately that the keys were the set she and Mitch had found at scene of the hit and run. Jordan reached down, picked up the keys and handed them back to Mitch.

"Thanks," Mitch mumbled.

If he had been looking for a flicker of recognition or a guilty reaction from Jordan Sloane, Cassie figured Mitch must have been disappointed. Cal Vantana's roommate hadn't given the keys a second glance.

As a hearty fire crackled and danced in the grate, Cassie's gaze traveled to three guns arranged in a decorative grouping over the mantel. One was either a shotgun or a rifle—she never had known the difference. The other two seemed to be antique pistols of some kind.

Cassie suppressed a shudder and looked away. She knew it was an overreaction, but ever since Brian's terrible death, the mere sight of a handgun or rifle had a chilling effect on her senses.

Sloane offered them coffee. Cassie started to respond, but Mitch spoke first, declining for both of them. Cassie shot him a withering glance.

"As I explained earlier," Mitch began, "I've got a few questions concerning your roommate."

Jordan Sloane shook his head and said doubtfully, "Well, I'll try to answer anything I can, but I'm not sure how much help I can be, if any. I was working Sunday when Cal had his accident."

Sloane had positioned himself in a worn leather chair across from them. He leaned forward, resting his elbows on his knees. "I hadn't known Cal very long," he said. "But I might be able to help locate his family, if that's the problem. Most men have a little black book." His eyes twinkled knowingly at Cassie. "Maybe Cal's had his family's address in it."

"That won't be necessary, Mr. Sloane," Mitch said tersely. "The sheriff's department has already located Vantana's sister in Phoenix."

Mitch was all business. As he continued to question Jordan Sloane about his relationship with Cal Vantana, Cassie couldn't help but wonder what had brought Cal to Denver and ultimately to his death. Friends? Family? Or another scam that would have ultimately sent him back to jail?

"And so you met Cal in a bar?" Mitch was saying when Cassie focused her attention back onto the conversation.

"It was pure chance," Jordan explained. "I work near the Goal Post. Have you heard of it?"

Mitch nodded. Cassie had driven by the popular downtown pub many times, and though she'd never been inside, she knew it was a busy sports bar.

"I play a little pool there on my days off. Catch a game on the big-screen TV. You know, hang out. Occasionally I meet a special lady for drinks," Jordan confided to Cassie with an easy smile.

It hadn't taken Cassie long to identify Jordan Sloane as a shameless flirt. Her sideways glance at Mitch told her he'd drawn the same conclusion. A tiny muscle in his jaw worked overtime as he gritted his teeth.

Grind away, Dempsey, she said to herself. *It serves you right.*

"Let's stick to the point, shall we?" Mitch suggested.

"Sorry," Sloane said apologetically.

"Exactly when and how did you meet Cal Vantana?" Mitch asked.

"I guess it was four, no maybe five weeks ago. I'd dropped by the Goal Post after work to catch the end of the Bronco game. I was still in uniform, come to think of it."

"Uniform? What do you do, Mr. Sloane?" Cassie asked.

"I'm an actor," he answered easily, giving her his best leading-man smile. "But between jobs I'm a chauffeur. The day I met Cal I was wearing my chauffeur's coat and cap."

Sloane went on to explain how he and Cal had played a few friendly games of pool before Cal, commenting on the chauffeur's uniform, approached Jordan about the possibility of getting a job as a driver.

"He said he was new in town, needed a job and was willing to do just about anything."

"And did you help him out?" Mitch asked.

"Sure, I tried to. I told him I didn't know if my boss was hiring, but that I'd check it out for him. I liked Cal, right away, you know? He was just that kind of person, real easygoing." As Jordan described Cal Vantana, his smile was sad and Cassie experienced a fresh twinge of guilt, feeling again that they were intruding on his loss.

Jordan went on to explain how he spoke with his employer the next day and set up a time for Cal to meet with her to apply for a part-time driving position.

"It could have worked out great," he said, shaking his head. "The job and the roommate situation, I mean. With the two of us working alternate shifts, we would never get in each other's way, you know? It could have all worked out."

"What else can you tell us about Cal Vantana?" Mitch asked. "Who were his friends? His enemies?"

"Enemies?" Jordan gave a dry laugh. "I can't imagine that Cal had anything but friends." His admiration for Cal seemed sincere, and Cassie began to wonder if Jordan Sloane was a more serious and thoughtful man than she had first judged him to be.

"Did he have any unusual interests?" Mitch asked.

Sloane's expression went blank. "Interests?"

"Any hobbies? Did he have a favorite sport or collect anything unusual?"

"You mean like stamps?"

"Or like classic cars," Mitch suggested.

Sloane's sudden laugh sliced the air. "Classic cars? Oh, no, I don't think so," he said, chuckling. "Outside of the clothes on his back and that old pickup, Cal didn't own much of anything else."

"Did you know he was an ex-con?" Mitch shot back quickly. If Mitch was trying to catch Sloane off balance, he'd succeeded, Cassie thought. She could almost hear his jaw when it dropped.

"What? Cal had been in jail? No way!"

"You didn't know about his prison record, then?" Mitch asked again.

"Absolutely not," Jordan insisted, rising and pacing closer to the fireplace. For a moment, he stood staring into the fire with his back to them.

"Wow. He lived under my roof and I didn't really know a thing about him." He spoke so softly it was almost as if he were talking to himself.

Running a hand through his thick crop of blond hair, he sighed deeply and sat back down. "When I think of what might have happened . . ."

"There's nothing to indicate Cal was a violent man," Mitch assured the obviously shaken man.

"But still, an ex-con! And I'm usually so careful. You know these are terrible times. The crime. The violence . . ."

"Well, at least you're well armed," Cassie blurted, indicating the guns above the mantel.

Sloane shook his head. "Oh, those. Inherited from my father. Wouldn't know how to use them if I had to."

When Mitch stood, Cassie followed suit. "Thank you, Mr. Sloane," Mitch said, extending his hand.

"You've been very helpful. Someone from the sheriff's department will be out sometime this week to collect Vantana's personal effects."

Jordan shook his head morosely. "Fine," he said as he followed them to the door.

"By the way, Cal's parole officer wasn't aware Cal had found a job yet. We'll need the name of his employer."

"Look, I don't want any trouble on my job," Sloane said uneasily.

"I'm sure your name won't even come up," Mitch assured him.

"Well, I suppose if you really need to have it—"

"I do," Mitch said firmly.

"I'm not sure if Cal had started to work, yet."

Cassie wondered why Jordan was hedging.

"Just give me the name," Mitch ordered.

"Grant Hahn," he blurted at last.

Cassie felt the blood drain from her face.

"Cal and I both drew our paychecks from him, but I take my orders from Lisa. I'm her personal driver. And Lisa would have been the one who hired Cal."

Chapter Ten

The shock of discovering a connection between her employer and Cal Vantana continued to wash over Cassie in small jolting waves. The next day, the tension and fatigue burned into her shoulders as she stretched to attach the last sugarplum fairy to the fishing line suspended from the ceiling of the display.

Climbing down from the ladder, she glanced at her watch. No wonder she felt drained. She and Mitch had mulled over their thoughts about the meeting with Jordan Sloane until after midnight last night. This morning, she'd been back at the store by eight. Now, it was after four and she'd been hard at it for over eight hours without a break.

Remembering the pop and candy machines in the employee lounge, Cassie grabbed her leather bag and stepped down out of the display. As she walked across the main floor, she heard someone calling her name.

"Cassie," the familiar female voice called out again.

Whirling around, Cassie spotted Lisa Hahn at the cosmetic counter, a large shopping bag and her coat tucked under her arm. Lisa's face was flushed as she hurried to catch up to her.

"Hello, Lisa," Cassie said, hoping the caution she instinctively felt toward Grant Hahn's wife didn't reflect in her voice.

"Going home?" Lisa asked.

"Hardly," Cassie said, shaking her head. "Just taking a break." Was Lisa's question an official inquiry? Cassie wondered bitterly.

"Sounds like a smart idea," Lisa agreed, her eyes shining. "Want some company?"

"I'm just going to the employee break room to grab a Coke."

"Ugh," Lisa groaned. "I never drink the stuff. Besides, that place will be jammed this time of day. Why don't we go upstairs? It'll be quieter."

Cassie hesitated, wondering if Lisa was merely being friendly or if she had some other reason for wanting to talk to her. Lisa seemed to sense her uncertainty.

"Oh, come on," she urged, looping her arm through Cassie's with easy familiarity. "We'll have a real drink. You know we haven't had a chance to talk since the day you came to lunch."

Cassie began to wonder if Lisa had conveniently forgotten that the conclusion of that luncheon hadn't exactly been amiable. Or maybe the couple of drinks Cassie suspected Lisa had already consumed this afternoon had dulled her memory?

A thought struck Cassie as they moved across the main floor toward the elevators. Maybe if Lisa felt relaxed and friendly, she'd also feel talkative. Perhaps their chance meeting could provide Cassie with some answers about Cal Vantana's connection to Hahn's.

"I'm afraid I'll have to pass on that drink. I still have quite a bit of work to do this evening. But if there's a Coke upstairs..."

"Oh, sure. Anything you want," Lisa boasted, still smiling as they stepped into the elevator and she punched the button for the penthouse.

"Grant told me about the accident in the displays." Lisa shook her head and frowned. "Rotten luck, huh?"

Cassie bit her lip. Luck? Accident? Was that the official word on the vandalism or merely how Grant had presented it to his wife?

In a moment, the elevator doors slid open onto the carpeted hallway of the executive floor. Cassie followed Lisa's lead as she headed toward the offices. Cassie's heart sank. When Lisa had said "upstairs" Cassie had assumed there was an executive break room.

Obviously Lisa wasn't aware of the tension that existed between her husband and Cassie. Her mind raced, trying to second-guess Lisa's true motives for insisting that Cassie accompany her to the executive offices.

"Where are we going?" Cassie asked uneasily.

"Grant's office, of course."

Cassie groaned inwardly. Grant Hahn was the last person she wanted to see right now. "Maybe I shouldn't have come...."

"Oh, don't be silly," Lisa said, a knowing smile lighting her face. "He left hours ago. Something about a meeting with the town council concerning the Crystal Creek development."

Lisa dropped her packages and her coat unceremoniously into a heap on the floor in the outer office and, after rummaging through her oversize bag for several moments, finally produced a key. With a triumphant, "Aha!" she shoved open the door and stepped into Grant's office.

"Come on," Lisa prodded when she saw Cassie hesitating.

Lisa crossed the spacious office to the wet bar and immediately poured herself a drink. Carrying the bottle in one hand and her glass in another, she plopped down into the butter-soft leather couch positioned across the room from her husband's desk.

"Sodas and ice are in there," she said, motioning to the small refrigerator behind her. "Help yourself."

After retrieving a can of Coke from the well-stocked refrigerator, Cassie perched uneasily on the edge of a chair.

Lisa kicked off her shoes and took a deep drink. "To my husband," she said, staring at his desk, a glint of anger reflected in her eyes.

Refilling her glass, Lisa rose and padded over to the long table that held the model of the Crystal Creek store. Cassie noticed Lisa's hand was wet. Her drink had sloshed over the side of her glass and drizzled onto the thick cream-colored carpet.

"Have you met my husband's first love, Cassie?" Lisa asked, staring down at the model. "Here, take a closer look," she beckoned. "She's really something. Quite a beauty, Grant's mistress."

Cassie was caught completely off guard by Lisa's behavior and her glib remarks.

"She's all he thinks about, you know?" Tipping her head, she drained the glass again. "Night and day.

She's the most important thing in his life." She stared down into her empty glass.

"After his family, of course," Cassie put in, feeling a surge of embarrassment and sympathy for Grant's wife.

"Of course," Lisa replied absently. "Hey, come on. Why don't you join me?" she asked, waving the bottle at Cassie. "Grant tells me this is the best little brandy money can buy. And he ought to know," she said, her sudden laughter sharp and shrill as she poured more of the amber liquid into her unsteady glass. "He's certainly bought enough of it trying to keep me happy."

Cassie said nothing as she watched Lisa head back toward the bar. Her steps were uncertain, and when she started to stumble, Cassie jumped up and reached out to steady her.

Lisa dismissed Cassie's assistance with a flip of her slim wrist. "I'm fine," she insisted, smiling, but even as she spoke, she turned and crashed into a small table. Cassie lunged to save a lamp from toppling over.

"Are you okay?" Cassie asked.

"Whoops! What a klutz I am." Lisa giggled, her speech slightly slurred and her eyes shining. "Happens all the time, you know? When you get to know me better, you'll understand."

Unfortunately, Cassie was already beginning to understand only too well. Lisa Hahn's life was way out of balance.

"Lisa, I really need to get back to work, now," Cassie said as she reached for her purse.

Lisa grabbed a fresh bottle of brandy and tucked it under her arm. "I gotta get goin' myself," she said, struggling into her shoes.

"Why don't I call someone to come get you?" Cassie suggested, feeling uncomfortable at the thought of Lisa driving herself home.

"Nope. Got a driver waiting downstairs."

"Your chauffeur?" Cassie asked, her interest piqued.

"Yeah," Lisa replied smiling. "Jordan." His name slid seductively off her tongue as she gathered her coat and bags off the floor.

Cassie followed her, feeling uneasy as she remembered her original motive for accepting Lisa's invitation to join her in the executive office. An innate sense of fair play argued with Cassie's need to know more about Jordan Sloane's and Cal Vantana's connection to the Hahn family.

"Is Jordan your only driver?" Cassie asked as they left the office together and headed toward the elevator. Lisa couldn't incriminate herself if she had nothing to hide, Cassie rationalized, trying to ease her own conscience.

Lisa's eyes sparkled. "Have you seen my driver, Cassie?" she asked in a coarse whisper. "With a chauffeur who looks like that, why would I want anyone else?" Her laughter resounded shrilly inside the elevator as the doors closed.

Cassie pushed the button for the main floor and decided to nudge Lisa a bit further. "I guess I see what you mean," she said, smiling. "I saw the limousine the day I came to the mansion and was just wondering if you had a professional service or one private chauffeur?''

Lisa's laughter died. Though definitely clouded by the effects of the alcohol, her intelligent eyes blinked to an unexpected alertness. "Now why would you be interested in knowing something like that, Cassie?" Lisa's tone was surprisingly sober.

"Did Cal Vantana ever drive for you, Lisa?" Cassie asked. "Did he drive for you last Sunday?" *The night he was killed,* Cassie added to herself with a shudder of remembrance.

Lisa stared back at her, unflinching. "What? Cassie, I don't know what you're talking about. My driver's name is Jordan. Jordan Sloane," she repeated slowly. "And as for Sunday night, I...was at home. All night. Home with Grant and Brandon."

"But you knew Cal Vantana, didn't you?"

Lisa's eyes clouded over again. "I—I did hire a part-time driver, but I don't remember his name. I've never been very good with names. Am I *supposed* to know him? Is he a friend of yours, Cassie?"

Cassie fixed her stare on Lisa's innocent expression. "He's the man who died outside of Hahn's Sunday night, Lisa. The man I saw deliberately run down." Just saying the words made Cassie's stomach churn.

Lisa's expression was pained as she shook her head and ran her fingers through her thick blond curls. "Oh, please, Cassie. Let's not get into all of that again—that hit-and-run business. I thought we'd settled all that," she said with an impatient wave of one hand. Her speech had become badly slurred again, and although she appeared to be telling the truth about not recognizing Cal Vantana's name, Cassie's instincts told her Lisa was stalling for time.

"Vantana," Cassie prodded. "Cal Vantana. He came to you looking for a job. Please try to remember, Lisa. It's very important."

Before Cassie could press Lisa further, the doors slid open and the tall, lithe frame of Jordan Sloane filled the opening.

The dark brown chauffeur's uniform he wore made Cassie gasp. It was the same kind of uniform Cal Vantana had worn the night he'd died.

"Mrs. Hahn!" Jordan exclaimed, smiling. He moved aside as Cassie and Lisa stepped out of the elevator.

"I've been all over the building trying to find you." His reproach was gentle and his expression was warm and admiring.

"Take these, will you, Jordan?" Lisa handed him her shopping bag and coat.

"I've got to go now, Cassie," she said. "Thanks for the company," she said without looking back.

Jordan acknowledged Cassie with a friendly smile as he turned to follow his employer. "Nice to see you again, Ms. Craig."

Cassie stared after them for a few seconds and then on impulse decided to follow them out of the building.

"You know he'll be furious if you're late for dinner again," Cassie overheard Jordan saying. "Why do you do this? It only makes things more difficult."

Cassie stopped near the time clock and watched them as they walked out the employee exit. Just before the door swung closed behind them, she saw Jordan Sloane slip his arm around Lisa's waist.

IMMERSED IN THOUGHT, Cassie headed back to the displays, her mind a jumble of unanswered questions. What was the real relationship between Jordan and Lisa? Why had Lisa denied knowing Cal Vantana?

"Now there goes a man who could drive me anywhere."

Cassie jerked around at the sound of Arlene's voice behind her. "What?"

"Lisa's chauffeur," Arlene said, her eyebrows lifted knowingly.

"You know him?" Cassie asked, falling into step beside the tall brunette.

"Don't I wish! I hear he's just inches away from his big break. He's an actor, you know." Arlene's eyes shone with excitement. "But unfortunately he's already got a girlfriend."

"Who?" Cassie asked, following Arlene as she pushed through the door of the employee break room. The room was empty except for two women sitting at a small metal table. Arlene made her way over to them, past the vending machines that lined the wall.

"Are you kidding?" Arlene asked as they sat down.

Cassie shook her head.

"I'll give you a big hint, you just saw them together." Arlene's smile was an unattractive sneer.

"Lisa and her driver?" asked the pudgy redhead sitting next to Cassie. "Are they at it again?"

"She's too tacky for words!" The latest comment came from the well-dressed, middle-aged lady sitting across from Arlene. Cassie remembered being introduced to Gretta Simmons, the assistant manager in ladies' sportswear.

"Why her husband puts up with her is a mystery to me," Arlene declared, her voice low and indignant. "A man like that deserves better."

Gretta and the redhead nodded their agreement.

"After all he's gone through with her...footing the tab for her scrapes with the law, raising her son while she checks in and out of those fancy rehab places."

Cassie disliked gossip and usually had no qualms about removing herself from its source, but in this instance she was all ears. "Lisa's had legal trouble?"

"I heard she's lost her driver's license for good this time," Gretta said, shaking her head disapprovingly.

"Does Grant know...about Lisa and Jordan, I mean?" Cassie asked tentatively.

The three women exchanged speculative glances. The redhead shrugged and shook her head. "I doubt it," she said. "If my Joe even suspected something like that about me, I'd be out on my ear."

"Oh, Pat, of course he knows," Gretta said emphatically. "If he knows everything that goes on around here, he surely knows what goes on in his own home."

"You're probably right," Patty agreed solemnly. "And you can be sure if Mr. Hahn didn't figure it out on his own, Arthur would be more than happy to clue him in. But it's just hard to believe he lets it go on."

"According to Doris in lingerie," Arlene said confidedly, "she not only subsidizes Jordan's acting lessons, but tried to convince Grant to invest in his career, as well.''

"I saw them together once—Mr. Hahn and Jordan," Gretta added. "They were outside arguing in the parking lot. For a moment I thought they were going to exchange blows."

"What happened?" Cassie asked.

"They saw me watching and they backed off. But I think if Mr. Hahn had had his way Jordan Sloane would have been history."

A grim theory of murder by mistaken identity began to form in the back of Cassie's mind. Had Cal Vantana been killed merely for the uniform he'd worn the night of the hit and run? Cassie gave herself a mental shake. Somehow the image of the cool and controlled Grant Hahn running a man down in a fit of jealous rage was just too unlikely to consider seriously.

"They say when he finally lets go, he has a terrible temper," Patty offered, tugging Cassie out of her dark introspection. "And that he's a very jealous man."

"Lord knows she's given him enough reason," Arlene added, rolling her eyes dramatically. "Gretta, you remember that young manager from the Salt Lake store they brought over to train with Arthur last year?"

Gretta nodded. "Lisa was all over him from his first day. Grant had Arthur fire him the second week."

"Excuse me, ladies."

The female voice behind them made Cassie jump. She hadn't realized anyone else was in the room. Ruth Palmer stood over them, glaring indignantly.

"It's nearly five. Shouldn't you all be back on the sales floor by now getting ready to close?"

"On my way," Arlene said dutifully, rolling her eyes at Cassie as she rose.

"Sorry, Ruth," Gretta and Patty said at the same time.

Cassie started to get up and follow the three women as they walked toward the door.

"Wait, Cassie," Ruth said. "Stay a minute, won't you? I want to talk to you."

Cassie sat back down. Ruth took the chair Arlene had vacated.

When the door closed and they were left alone, Ruth laced her hands in front of her on the table and took a deep breath. "Break room gossip is a fact of life at Hahn's," she said evenly. "You shouldn't believe everything you hear, Cassie. Grant and Lisa are young, good-looking, and members of Denver's social elite. I'm afraid that makes them fair game for the kind of talk you heard today."

Cassie nodded. "Then you're saying that what they told me isn't true?"

Ruth was silent for a moment before she pushed the chair away from the table and rose. "What I'm saying," she said carefully, "is that I'm glad Grant Hahn is my employer. He's a fine, decent man with a lot of people depending on him. Mrs. Hahn, well, as you already know, Lisa has had her problems," Ruth said quietly, her eyes downcast. "But she is his wife and I try to respect her." Cassie saw regret in Ruth's expression.

Ruth walked to the door. "Do yourself a favor, Cassie. Just do your work. Finish the holiday windows and stay out of Grant Hahn's personal life. He has worked long and hard to make Hahn's the success it is. The Crystal Creek store is his dream now, and if I can help it, no one is going to spoil it for him. No one."

Cassie sat in stunned silence for a moment after Ruth left the room. Her parting words had been an undisguised threat. Ruth's devotion to Grant Hahn was total, Cassie realized. She'd made his dreams her own. Did Ruth view Cassie as a threat to those dreams? And if she did, just how far would she go to protect them?

Walking back to the displays, Ruth Palmer's words echoed through Cassie's mind. She wondered if Grant Hahn knew how his secretary felt about him. Cassie wished with all her heart she could heed Ruth's sound advice to forget about the lives of Grant and Lisa Hahn and get on with completing the job she'd been contracted to do. How much simpler and safer her own life would be.

Chapter Eleven

An hour later, when Arlene stuck her head around the corner of the display, Cassie jumped.

"Sorry, kiddo," Arlene said. "I didn't mean to frighten you."

"Is the store closing?" Cassie had been so absorbed in her work and her thoughts she hadn't noticed the time.

Arlene nodded. "What a day. Well, I just wanted to say good-night and give you this." She stepped up into the displays and handed Cassie a note. "The switchboard put this call through to my counter a few minutes ago. I offered to come get you, but he said just to give you the message." Arlene's eyes sparked with delighted curiosity. "Mitch? Isn't that your hunky cop?"

Cassie smiled and lowered her eyes to read her message.

Found our ghost. Call me. Love, Mitch.

"Thanks, Arlene," Cassie said, scooping up purse and jacket.

"A ghost?" Arlene asked, following Cassie out of the displays. "What does that mean?"

"I wish I knew," Cassie replied as she hurried around the nearest cosmetic counter and reached for the phone. "Can I use this?"

Arlene shook her head. "You won't be able to get an outside line. The switchboard closed ten minutes ago. The only phone with an outside line after hours is the one on the wall next to the employee exit."

Cassie remembered the phone well, and was hurrying toward it even before Arlene told her. It was the same phone she'd used the night of the hit and run.

"What's going on, Cassie?" Arlene persisted, trying to keep up as Cassie hurried toward the employee exit. "Are you in some kind of trouble?"

"Everything's fine," Cassie assured her. "But I've got to go," Cassie explained, deciding as she walked that she'd have to make her call elsewhere if she wanted privacy. "See you tomorrow. Thanks for taking the message," she said as she hurried through the exit.

"See you tomorrow." Arlene's words drifted out the door behind her, but Cassie barely heard them. Her thoughts were fastened firmly on a single goal: talking to Mitch and finding out what he'd discovered. Had Mitch found the car whose keys might have cost Cal Vantana his life?

Cassie's thoughts raced as she slipped the key into the ignition and gunned the engine to life. Shoving the Honda into reverse, Cassie glanced in the rearview mirror and started to back up.

When a set of headlights speared the darkness, Cassie stomped on the brakes to avoid a collision with the car coming toward her. Relief broke over her as she recognized the car swinging into the space next to her as Mitch's Porsche.

She watched him climb out of his car, and she suppressed a sigh. The dome light reflected his smile as he opened her door and slid into the seat beside her. The navy blue cable-knit sweater he wore made his eyes seem an even deeper shade of blue.

"I'm glad I caught you," he said. "If we hurry we won't be late."

"Arlene gave me your message. I was just on my way home to call."

"Let's go," he said. "Do you know the fastest way to the Denver Country Club area?"

"Sure." She nodded. The exclusive country club district wasn't far from where the new Crystal Creek Mall was under construction. "Mitch, what's this all about?"

He put his arm across the back of the seat and gave her a quick hug. "I think we may have found it, Cass. The missing piece to our puzzle. Now step on it," he ordered smiling. "We've got a date with a ghost and we don't want to be late."

As CASSIE DROVE, Mitch explained how he'd tried to speed up their search for the Silver Ghost.

"I figured there couldn't be that many of the rare classics in the area and that the collectors' organizations would be the logical place to begin our search."

First, he'd obtained a list of all the classic auto clubs in town from a dealer. Next, he'd located and contacted some officers of those clubs.

"It was easy to get them to talk about the automobiles their clubs had been formed around," Mitch said. "The Silver Ghost was a model built during the years 1906 to 1925. The 1921s are extremely rare and especially valued for their elegant body styling."

As Cassie signaled to make a right and pulled out onto Sixth Avenue, Mitch went on to explain how acquiring information about the owners, specifically names and addresses, hadn't been easy. "The owners of these classics are often very wealthy and very private people," Mitch explained. "Often, they have a small fortune tied up in the restoration and maintenance of their classics."

"Theft must be a very real concern," Cassie interjected.

"Exactly. I've been considering an alarm for the Porsche for that very reason."

As it turned out, the Porsche had aided Mitch in his inquiries. Seeing the classic sports car had finally convinced one officer of a collectors' club that Mitch's inquiries were legitimate.

"I figured we were still days, maybe weeks, away from obtaining names and addresses. But we got lucky," Mitch told her. "The historian of the Rolls club in Lakewood was very interested in the 911. When I promised to contact him first if I ever decided to sell her, he was more than willing to offer his assistance."

"You're not seriously considering selling the Porsche, are you?"

Mitch smiled and shook his head. "Anyway, finally, by comparing the Motor Vehicle printout and the list of names I obtained from the historian, I struck pay dirt. Turns out there are only two Silver Ghost owners registered in the Denver area and the historian had the names of both.''

"That's terrific," Cassie exclaimed.

"The first owner I tried to contact is a professor at C.U., but unfortunately he's on sabbatical in England for the next twelve months."

Cassie sighed her disappointment.

"But I spoke with the other owner, a Mrs. Marjorie Bayless. She informed me that her Rolls was not for sale and started to hang up on me until I mentioned the historian's name. That must have given me some credibility, because she agreed to see us this evening."

"Did you ask her about Cal Vantana?"

Mitch shook his head. "If she does know anything about him or his death, I didn't want to spook her."

In a few minutes, Cassie wheeled the Honda off the main road into a private driveway that curved through the trees and ended in front of a spacious residence that bespoke its owner's wealth. Cassie noted the four-car garage north of the house, and excitement bubbled inside her.

"Just think, we're finally getting to see our Ghost," she said, smiling. Mitch gave her hand a reassuring squeeze as they jogged up the front stairs.

At the door, they were greeted by Mrs. Bayless, who showed them into a well-appointed library just off the large open entryway.

"Thank you for seeing us on such short notice, Mrs. Bayless," Mitch said. As he spoke, Cassie watched Mrs. Bayless fuss with the gray curls that framed her round face, and wondered if any woman was immune to the Dempsey charm.

"Oh, I'm always eager to assist those as interested in the Rolls as Seth and I were," she said brightly.

"Were?" Cassie asked, her heart sinking. Did Marjorie Bayless mean she and her husband no longer owned the Silver Ghost?

"I'm a widow," Mrs. Bayless explained softly.

Mitch and Cassie uttered their apologies and then listened intently as Mrs. Bayless went on to explain in detail her husband's lifelong passion for antique autos.

Cassie found her mind begin to wander as she tried to think of a way to introduce Cal's name into the conversation.

"When Seth died, I sold the Stutz and the Bentley," Mrs. Bayless was saying when Cassie's attention drifted back to her. "But the Rolls was his favorite, and so far I just haven't been able to let it go." The older woman's glistening eyes told Cassie that parting with the Silver Ghost would mean parting with more memories of the husband to whom she'd been so obviously devoted.

For a moment Marjorie Bayless fell silent. When she settled her gaze on Cassie for a lingering moment, Cassie smiled despite the intense scrutiny that was becoming more and more uncomfortable. "Miss Craig, I get the distinct feeling we've met? Are you from the Denver area?"

Cassie nodded uneasily; if Mrs. Bayless was a regular Hahn's customer, she might remember Cassie from the department store. "Yes," she replied honestly. "I've lived here almost all my life."

The older woman's face broke into a relieved smile. "I thought you looked familiar. Maybe I've seen you at the country club. Do you play tennis? Golf, maybe?"

Cassie shook her head. "I don't belong to any country clubs, Mrs. Bayless," she said. Though it was true Cassie was a Denver native, the neighborhood where she'd grown up was a long way both geographically and economically from the exclusive Denver Country Club section of town.

"Has the car been in the family a long time?" Mitch asked, steering the conversation back in the direction of the Silver Ghost.

"Oh, heavens, no," Mrs. Bayless exclaimed, shaking her head. "Seth had purchased the car just six months before his death. That would be almost three years ago, now," she explained wistfully. "But he did have his eye on it for a long, long time."

"At a dealership?" Mitch prodded.

"What? Oh, no...actually a friend owned the Ghost before we did."

"A Mr. Vantana?" Cassie blurted.

Mitch scowled, but Mrs. Bayless only stared vacantly at her. "Why, no. Is Mr. Vantana a Rolls collector?"

If Marjorie Bayless did have some prior knowledge of Cal Vantana, indeed if she'd ever even heard his name before this moment, Cassie thought she did a great job of faking it. "No..." Cassie stammered. "He-he's just a friend I thought you might know."

Mitch shot her a look that screamed caution.

"As you were saying, Mr. Bayless finally convinced his friend to sell?" Mitch urged Marjorie Bayless back to the recounting of how they'd come to own the Ghost.

"Yes, my Seth could be a very persuasive man," she said beaming. "Grant's father had left him the Ghost—though I don't really think it ever meant as much to him as it did to Seth," she confided as an afterthought.

"Grant? Grant Hahn?" Cassie exclaimed.

"Why, yes," Mrs. Bayless answered, her soft brown eyes narrowing. "Grant Hahn. Do you know him?"

Cassie could barely contain herself. The implications of the Hahn connection to the Silver Ghost sent her thoughts swirling. "Grant Hahn is my boss," Cassie admitted.

"Your boss?" Mrs. Bayless said thoughtfully, her voice fading.

"Mrs. Bayless," Mitch broke in, "did you take the Rolls out on Sunday night?"

"What's this all about?" Mrs. Bayless asked uneasily. "I thought you were a collector, Mr. Dempsey."

"We just have a few questions, ma'am," Mitch said, rising. "We have reason to believe that your vehicle may be involved somehow in a crime that was committed last Sunday in front of Hahn's department store."

Marjorie Bayless looked stricken as she rose to her feet. "I think you'd better go now." Her voice had an icy edge. "Both of you. The Hahn's are old and dear family friends and I wouldn't do anything to hurt any of them."

"But Mrs. Bayless..."

Marjorie Bayless brushed past Cassie and strode dramatically out of the room without looking back. Mitch took Cassie's hand. They had no choice but to follow Mrs. Bayless to the door.

"But all we want to do is to take a look at the car," Cassie explained.

"Absolutely not." Her stare flicked between them. "You came here under false pretenses, and now I must insist that you leave my home at once before I call the police."

Mitch put his hand on Cassie's back and moved toward the open door. "Mrs. Bayless, I am a policeman, a detective with the Denver Police Department. I apologize for the intrigue. We meant no harm. If you could just let us take a look at the car tonight it might avoid a difficult legal situation later."

The older woman's resolve seemed to waver a moment. Her eyes darted uncertainly between them. "Mr. Dempsey—or whatever your real name is," she said suspiciously, "the Rolls has not been moved out of the garage since my husband died. Therefore it is not possible that it was involved in anything illegal."

"Just one more question, do you still have the keys to the Rolls, Mrs. Bayless?" Mitch asked from the doorstep.

"Of course I do," she snapped. "Why wouldn't I?"

"Could I see them please?" Mitch said.

"Not without a warrant!" Mrs. Bayless snapped. "And now, if there are any more questions, I suggest you contact my attorney." The door was politely but firmly closed in their faces.

A moment later, when they were back out on the road, Cassie asked, "Can you do that, Mitch? Get a warrant to make Marjorie Bayless produce the keys to the Rolls?"

Mitch shook his head. "As far as the Denver PD is concerned, the Cal Vantana file is closed, remember?"

"But it's all just too darned coincidental. Cal Vantana's connection to Lisa, and now this. Mitch, we've got to get a look at that car," Cassie insisted. "If the keys we found at the scene of the hit and run fit the Silver Ghost..."

"I know," he said, running his fingers through his thick dark hair. "I know."

Cassie recognized the contemplative tone of his voice and knew he was searching for a way around their dilemma. Her own thoughts were busy sorting scenarios faster than she could process them all.

The Bayless's 1921 Silver Ghost had once belonged to Grant Hahn. A key chain with a valuable replica of the Silver Ghost had been in Cal Vantana's possession moments before his murder. His death had been made to look like an accident. According to Jordan Sloane, Cal Vantana had been hired as a part-time driver by Lisa Hahn. If the keys found at the scene of the hit and run fit Bayless's Rolls-Royce—as Cassie believed they would—the connection between Cal Vantana and Grant and Lisa Hahn was complete.

But then what? What did it all mean? Cassie asked herself impatiently. Where did the bizarre connection between the department store magnate, his wife and an ex-con lead them? And what was the point of any of this conjecture if they could never be sure?

A few moments later, Cassie steered her Honda into the space next to Mitch's car in the deserted parking garage. Shutting off the engine, she turned to him.

"What now?" she asked wearily.

"You're going home," he said flatly. "And I'm going back to the Bayless mansion."

She started to protest, but he pressed a finger gently to her lips. "No arguments," he said firmly. "I'll call you in the morning and let you know what I've learned."

Cassie pushed his hand away. "I'm going with you," she informed him, trying to ignore the circle of caresses his thumb swirled around her fist.

"No way, Cass," he said.

"Listen, Mitch. I think I should call Mrs. Bayless, explain to her what happened—what I saw, maybe she'll give me another chance to explain. I think I might be able to reason with her, convince her to let us at least take a look at the Rolls."

"As I recall, her mind seemed pretty closed to the subject when we left," Mitch reminded her.

"But maybe if I go back without you, without the threat you represent as a cop, I can change her mind. I really don't think you'll have a chance of reaching her, Mitch."

"But you don't understand," he said. "I'm not going back to try to convince her of anything. I'm going back tonight to find a way into that garage to get a look at the Silver Ghost and to see if our keys fit."

Cassie felt her heart thudding against her chest and she jerked her hand away from his grip. "I'm going with you."

His mouth set in a rigid line. "No way, Cass. Your career's already hanging on the line. One more misstep with Hahn's and you're out."

"Oh, and I suppose you're in a better position?" she challenged. "You're a cop, Mitch. Remember? You're supposed to uphold the law, not break it! If caught breaking into that garage, I'm only looking at losing a contract and dealing with some unpleasant legalities, but you, why, your whole career could be ruined."

"And since when are you interested in me and my career?" He stared at her, his incredible eyes simmering with blue heat.

"Since always," she shot back.

Without warning, he reached for her, and without a second thought she moved willingly into his embrace. The effects of her admission and his sensual presence sent a quiver of electric anticipation sizzling through her.

"I'm going with you," she repeated with as much authority as her trembling senses allowed. "Now tell me what to do."

Slowly he released her and leaned back to study her face. In the darkness, the tension crackled between them like lightning across a startled midnight sky.

"I don't like this, Cass," he said, his voice steely. "You could get hurt."

"I'm not worried," she teased with forced brightness. "You're a cop, aren't you? It's your job to protect me."

THE SOFT GLOW of light coming from inside the Bayless mansion shone through the thick border of pine and juniper and cast writhing shadows around the windbreak that surrounded and provided privacy for the estate.

Cassie tried to keep from stumbling, hurrying to keep up with Mitch's athletic movements as he wound his way through the trees toward the garage. A brisk night wind mixed with her own mounting apprehension sent a series of nervous shivers skating down her spine.

"Stay down," Mitch whispered as he reached for her hand and pulled her up next to where he was crouched on the ground.

They'd already arrived at the end of the windbreak and the end of their cover, Cassie realized. Another step and they'd be exposed to the neat row of footlights that lined the sides of the driveway and illuminated the front of the four-car garage.

Only a few hundred feet away, the north side of the structure stood dappled in windswept shadows. Mitch motioned for Cassie to stay put as he dashed across the driveway. In seconds, he slipped into the darkness on the far side of the large stone building.

Cassie stifled a shriek when a pebble landed at her feet, and quickly realized Mitch was signaling her to follow him. Imitating his crouching motions, Cassie hurried across the driveway. Her tennis shoes made no sound as she ran for the thick shadows where moments before she'd seen Mitch disappear.

Her eyes still hadn't adjusted to the darkness when she heard him whisper, "So far so good."

"How do we get in?" she asked breathlessly, moving up closer beside him.

Taking her hand, he pulled her with him as he edged toward the back of the garage. Just past a pile of neatly stacked lumber, Cassie spied a door. Suddenly her hopes soared, but just as quickly they were dashed when she saw the door was padlocked. Mitch muttered a colorful expletive under his breath.

"Can we break in?"

"Probably," he said, and pulled a small metal case out of his pocket.

"Wait," Cassie said, pointing to a series of wires she spotted running along the door frame.

"A security system. I should have known," Mitch said angrily. "If I try to pick that lock all hell could break loose."

"What's that?" Cassie said, pointing to something dark attached to the lower half of the door.

Together they knelt down and examined the heavy rubber attachment. "It's our ticket inside, Cass," Mitch said smiling. "A doggie door."

Without warning, he planted a quick kiss on her cheek. Despite the realization that they'd just crossed over one more emotional boundary, Cassie basked in the feeling of shared triumph that passed between them.

But her smile faded when she stopped to contemplate the size of the animal the pet entry had been designed to accommodate.

"What do you think?" he asked.

"I think I can get through. No problem," she said, folding back the rubber flaps and peering into the darkness on the other side of the opening. "But you'll never make it."

"Forget it, then," Mitch said sharply. "We'll have to find some other way."

"Give me the keys," Cassie demanded.

"No way, Cass. You're not going in there alone."

"Listen, Mitch, we haven't got time to argue. Don't you get it? It's probably better this way. One person will make less noise than two. And you can stay out here behind the lumber pile and keep watch. If anyone comes near, you can warn me and we'll make a run for it."

Even in the darkness Cassie could feel the heat from his blue-eyed gaze as it swept over her. "No way, Cass," he said again. "I just can't let you do it."

"Fine," she snapped angrily. "Have it your way, Dempsey, but we're liable to make a whole lot of noise when I wrestle you for those damn keys."

His silence told her he didn't feel particularly threatened.

"Come on, Mitch," she urged. "What other choice do we have?" she whispered urgently. "We're here. Let's go for it."

She heard a soft jingling sound as he pulled the keys from his pocket, and in the next moment she felt the cool metal in her palm.

"Once you're inside, stay down," he instructed. "If you move into the light, you could trigger an alarm."

"Right," Cassie said, her voice sounding a bit thin.

"The gearbox should be fairly simple to find. Just see if any of the keys fit and then, for God's sake, get the hell out of there."

She nodded, her throat gone too dry to speak. But even if she had managed to find her voice, it would have done her no good, for her lips were suddenly immobilized by his quick, hot kiss.

"Now get going," he ordered. "And be careful."

With the taste of his kiss still clinging to her lips, Cassie wriggled through the rubber-lined pet door. Easing her head and shoulders and finally her hips and legs through the opening was relatively easy. But she'd been right, Mitch's broad shoulders would never have made it through.

"I thought you said you'd gained weight," she heard his whispered accusation from the other side.

"I lied." She imagined his wry grin and it gave her the confidence to go on.

Moving away from the door and deeper into the spacious garage, Cassie remembered Mitch's instructions and kept her head and shoulders low, moving in a crouched position along the side of the car parked in the first stall.

A sporty convertible, sleek and modern, was something Cassie would have stopped to admire under different circumstances, but of absolutely no interest to her at the moment.

The next vehicle was a late-model town car. The long sedan was a glossy silver. It was luxurious, expensive looking and sophisticated. For a moment, Cassie imagined the fair-haired Jordan Sloane behind the wheel in his chauffeur's uniform. She studied the sedan a moment longer under the half-light that filtered through the windows lining the top third of the garage doors behind her. The town car was a beautiful automobile but definitely not an antique, Cassie realized with disappointment.

Creeping along the back of the town car, Cassie's attention suddenly flew to the magnificent automobile parked next to it.

The Silver Ghost! There could be no mistake. It truly was one of a kind. Its lustrous chrome glistened in the soft light. From the delicate winged lady gracefully perched on the hood, to the gentle rise of the rear fenders, everything about the Silver Ghost whispered elegance. No wonder Seth Bayless had treasured this car above all his other possessions.

Suddenly Cassie was struck by the startling resemblance between the small replica on the key chain she clutched in her hand and the real thing. Remembering the charm and the keys jolted her into action. Quickly she moved up alongside the Rolls, looking for the gearbox. As Mitch had predicted, it was easy to find. Locating the keyhole was another matter. Cassie strained her eyes in the dim light and finally found it.

She soon realized she should have singled out the odd key before she'd reached the garage and marked it somehow so that she could find it easily in the half-light. She was making too much noise and wasting too much time, she warned herself.

"Come on," she whispered as she tried to slip the first key into the slot. But to her chagrin, she found no matter how many different ways she turned it, the key refused to fit. Cassie felt a knot of disappointment tightening in the pit of her stomach when she discovered that the second key didn't fit, either.

As she fumbled with the last key, Cassie thought she detected a movement in front of the Rolls. She froze.

"Mitch?" she called out in a choked whisper. "Is that you?"

For a full moment, Cassie remained motionless. Her nerves must be playing tricks on her, she decided as she focused her attention back on the last key. Her heart sank when it refused to be shoved into the lock.

With trembling hands, Cassie turned the key over and tried again. This time her efforts were rewarded. The key slid easily and completely into the lock. A perfect fit!

"Yes!" Her victorious exclamation was a muffled shriek. Cassie stayed low and moved quickly as she edged her way past the town car and around the convertible. She couldn't wait to get to Mitch and share her success.

But her feelings of triumph were cut short when she heard a low, rumbling sound behind her. This was no case of nerves. Something had made that sound, something alive, and judging by the sound she heard again, something moving closer.

Cassie eased slowly around the back of the convertible toward the pet door. Out of the corner of her eye, she saw another movement. A low, menacing sound made the skin on the back of her neck prickle, and it felt as though the blood froze in her veins as terrifying reality dawned. The vicious growl and the creature who'd made it were right behind her.

Chapter Twelve

Turning around slowly, Cassie's gasped when she saw the shining yellow eyes of the huge black dog not five feet away from her and drawing nearer.

She glanced around desperately for a possible weapon, but her heart sank when she saw that there was nothing. The dog was edging closer, crouched in a challenge. Its growling warning grew louder, more meaningful, its eyes glinted hatred, its fangs bared.

Without turning her back to the animal, Cassie took a cautious step sideways and backward. "It's okay, boy," she muttered, trying to assure herself and the animal.

"It's okay. Good boy. I was just leaving," she uttered in a small shaky voice, her courage cracking.

The urge to turn tail and run for her life was nearly overwhelming, but she'd heard somewhere that you should never show an animal your fear. Show him, hell! This animal would have to be half-dead or completely senile not to have sensed the terror seeping from her every pore.

Cassie inched closer to the pet door. The dog continued its low rumbling. He hunched forward, his shoulder muscles quivering, his powerful hind legs ready to lunge.

At last, Cassie felt the stiff rubber lining of the pet door directly behind her. If the dog was going to attack, Cassie figured it was now or never.

With speed and agility she never knew she possessed, Cassie dropped to the ground and scampered through the pet door backward. She didn't know if she imagined it, or if the dog was really right behind her, but later, she swore she remembered feeling his hot breath on her face.

"No!" she yelled as she backed out of the opening, and amazingly the animal shrank back, momentarily stunned by her sudden show of authority.

Cassie felt Mitch's hands on her as he helped her to her feet. "There's a giant dog in there!" she exclaimed, grabbing his arm. "Let's get out of here."

"Right behind you, beautiful," Mitch said, "but first let's slow Fido down." He grabbed a board from the lumber pile and wedged it tightly across the opening.

The sound of frenzied barking told them the dog had tried to come after them and had discovered his path blocked. Without looking back, Cassie ran hand in hand with Mitch through the windbreak. Ignoring the branches that scraped and tore at their clothing, they zigged and zagged blindly through the trees.

Out on the road, they broke into a run as the cold night air carried the sounds of frenzied barking, angry voices and urgent footsteps running after them.

HALF AN HOUR LATER, Cassie still shivered as she huddled on her sofa. Trying to coax all the warmth she could into her frozen fingertips, she wrapped her hands around a steaming mug of hot chocolate. Mitch sat down beside her and pulled a soft down-filled quilt over their legs.

"Feeling better?" he asked as he took a tentative sip from his own mug before setting it down onto the coffee table.

"Much," Cassie replied, nodding. "For a minute back there I thought I might be the entrée on Rover's midnight menu."

Mitch laughed and the sound sent a flood of warmth flowing through her that proved much more effective than the hot chocolate in chasing her chills away. It felt so good, so right to be near him again.

"I wish I could have seen your face when that key slipped into the lock."

"I was as surprised as I was elated. But what does it all mean, Mitch?" she asked seriously. "Do you think Marjorie Bayless is involved in some way with Cal Vantana's murder?"

He shook his head. "Aside from the Silver Ghost, there's no real connection between them. I'm much more inclined to go for the obvious connection between Vantana and Grant Hahn."

"But is it enough to convince your chief to launch a murder investigation?"

"Hardly," Mitch admitted. "I'm afraid all our midnight escapade proved was our own hunches."

She shivered again, her body still reacting to the memory of the gruesome hit and run that had settled like a winter chill bone-deep inside her. Mitch took the cup from her hands and pulled the comforter tighter around them both.

His arm slipped around her under the quilt. Cassie leaned into his warmth, ignoring the warning bells going off in her head.

"Getting warmer," he asked, his mouth dangerously close to her ear.

"Hmm."

"I've missed you, Cassie," he whispered her name as his lips feathered kisses along that sensitive spot beneath her earlobe. "So much."

Words could never express just how much she'd missed him, Cassie told herself. How much she missed moments like this, the good times.

If still loving Mitch was so wrong, she asked herself, then why did it feel so right to be in his arms? Why did she still thrill to the sensual promises his lips made at the nape of her neck?

She remembered the good times and her heart swelled. But could she erase that other past, that terrible time that tore them apart? Was she willing to just forget how deeply he'd hurt her? Was she willing to forgive?

Cassie closed her eyes and let a gentle murmur of delight escape moments before his mouth moved over hers, and his lips began to make love to her in slow, tender caresses.

"Yes," she whispered, answering her own questions and shutting out all other thoughts except for the loving sensations his touch evoked inside her. In his arms, anything could be forgotten, anything forgiven.

Anything but the ringing telephone! Cassie's mind registered as the incessant sound tugged her away from him.

"Forget it," Mitch insisted in a gruff whisper as he pulled her into his arms. "They'll call back in the morning."

Cassie longed to agree, but the late hour of the call made her feel especially uneasy. What if it was an emergency? Something might have happened to someone in her family.

"I can't," she apologized as she pulled out of his embrace and hurried to the wall phone in the kitchen.

"Hello?" she said breathlessly. The voice on the other end of the line was vaguely familiar, but it took Cassie a few minutes to make the connection.

"Is this who I think it is?" Cassie demanded, her anger rising.

"Yes, it's me," Scott Avery answered. "Hey, I know it's late, but I drove by your place on the way home and I saw your lights were still on. Listen, we've got to talk. Have you thought any more about that follow-up story?"

"You've got a lot of nerve calling here," Cassie informed him tersely. "What makes you think I'd have anything else to say to you, Scott Avery?"

At the mention of the reporter's name, Mitch rose and moved over beside her.

"Hey, I know you weren't too crazy about that first article," Avery admitted, "but give me a break, it did get a response, didn't it?"

"If you call nearly losing my job a response . . ."

"I heard it got you a lot more than that," he interrupted. "I heard about the vandalism. Want to talk about it? It would make a great follow-up story, Cassie."

"Forget it, Avery," she snapped. "You've caused me nothing but trouble." Mitch touched her shoulder and nodded his agreement.

"Me?" Avery protested. "Honey, I'm only an innocent bystander. Just think about it, will you? That first article stirred somebody up, made them nervous enough to try to threaten you away from pursuing the truth about what you saw. Maybe a follow-up would push them out into the open."

"Maybe not," Cassie said skeptically, though she could glimpse a bit of logic in what he'd said. "How did you know about the vandalism? It wasn't reported to the police."

"Hey, I've got my sources," he said indignantly. "Now, what do you say to another interview?"

"I need to think about it," Cassie replied slowly.

"Take your time. Sleep on it," Avery suggested. "But the longer you wait, the longer the hit-and-run driver has to cover his trail. Here's my number. Call me in the morning."

Cassie scribbled the number on the back of a grocery receipt before she hung up the phone. She saw Mitch's eyes narrow and a furrow of concern crease his forehead and knew she didn't need to fill him in on the gist of her phone conversation with the *Herald* reporter.

"You're not going to do it." It wasn't a question. It was an order, and Cassie found Mitch's authoritative tone extremely irritating.

"I don't know yet," she countered quickly. "What he had to say made some sense."

"Cass, you can't even consider talking to that guy again."

"He could be right, you know. The vandalism was a warning. Another article could force the driver to act again, and this time maybe he'd slip up and reveal his identity."

He placed his hands on her shoulders and held her out at arm's length. "Cassie, I won't let you take any more risks. I'll talk to the chief in the morning about what we've learned tonight. We've made headway. Maybe I can convince him to reopen the investigation."

He released her and picked up the piece of paper with Scott Avery's phone number on it.

"Promise me you'll forget all about this follow-up article nonsense?"

"I can't do that." She snatched the paper from his hand. "You said yourself we have nothing but hunches," she reminded him. "And just how were you planning to tell your boss about our little breaking-and-entering episode this evening, Mitch?"

His reaction to her challenge was stony. "Why don't you let me worry about that?"

Cassie stared at him, her mind whirling around the possible content of the next news article. How far should she go in trying to bait the killer into the open?

"Damn it, Cass. I'm not getting through to you at all, am I?"

Impulsively she touched his cheek and watched the tension pulse around his strong jaw. "Oh, you're getting through to me, all right," she muttered, staring into his steel blue eyes and longing to give herself up completely to the crazy emotions that sexy gaze evoked. "But I've got to do what I think is right, Dempsey. Try to understand."

"No way," he said gruffly. "There's too much at stake. Give me his number. I'll call him in the morning and set him straight. I promise you when I'm through with him, Scott Avery will never bother you again."

His words had the effect of gasoline on an open flame. How could she have imagined he'd changed when times like this proved everything was the same? He still doubted her, doubted her ability to handle the obstacles life threw in her way. He was just as controlling and bullheaded as ever.

She'd been a fool to let her emotions get in the way, let her defenses down, let him grab hold of her heart again.

"Damn it, Mitch," she whispered, backing away to gain the distance she needed to say the words that formed a burning lump in her throat and squeezed her heart. "You have no right to decide what's right or wrong for me. You had no right then, and you have no right now! This is my decision. My call!" she insisted, her voice rising angrily. "My risk. And I'll be the one to decide if I should take it. You can't make the final decision this time, the way you did when you decided I couldn't hack it as a cop's wife."

The pain she saw in his eyes told her she'd exposed a nerve, but anger and pride forced her to stand firm.

"Is that what you thought?" he said, his voice low and hoarse.

She nodded, biting her lip against the stinging tears she'd be damned if she'd let him see. "You weren't very subtle, as I recall," she said bitterly, swiping at her eyes with the back of her hand.

He reached for her, but she jerked away from him.

"Cassie, listen to me. I never doubted you. It wasn't like that at all. But watching Holly after Brian died, seeing what she went through. How could I put you in that position? Don't you get it? I just couldn't let you take that chance."

"It wasn't your decision to make alone." Her voice was racked with two years of pain.

"I know that now and I've regretted it for a very long time," he said softly. "I was wrong. But I *have* changed. And I'll prove it to you. We can have that second chance, Cass. But not this way," he insisted. "I just can't let you take a stupid and dangerous risk."

Cassie stared at him, turmoil tearing at her heart. Every emotion inside her cried out for her to believe him. Who knew? Maybe there could be a second chance for them, after all. But if Mitch had truly changed, he'd have to start by proving it to her now.

She crumpled the paper in her hand. "It's late," she said quietly. "I think you'd better go."

He stared at her a long moment before he turned and walked to the door. "I'll call you tomorrow," he said.

She only nodded, finding that somehow she just couldn't say another word.

"I love you, Cassie Craig," he said at the door. "You love me. And you and I both know that's something that will never change."

IT HAD BEEN OVER twenty-four hours since she'd made her decision and now, as Cassie reread the article in this morning's paper, she felt she'd made a good one.

Scott Avery had kept his word. The follow-up article that claimed only a small corner of page forty-seven was an almost verbatim quote, reiterating that what she'd witnessed on the downtown sidewalk Sunday night still appeared to be a deliberate hit and run.

The article emphasized the fact that despite the police department's refusal to act, the *Herald* still wasn't prepared to let the matter drop and that the "witness" still held out hope that someone else might step forward to corroborate her story.

Cassie left the newspaper lying on the kitchen table and hurried into the bedroom. As she ran a brush through her shoulder-length hair, she wondered if Mitch had seen the article yet. A glance at the clock radio beside the bed told her she didn't have time to deal with his reaction if he called. She still had to change clothes and tend to Caruso before she left. If she hurried, she just might make it before Hahn's opened for business.

Cassie slipped into a comfortable pair of twill pants and tugged a pale blue sweater over her head as she rushed back into the kitchen. The small sherbet-colored canary was delighted to have his cage uncovered. As usual, he voiced his appreciation by serenading Cassie as she filled his water and seed cup.

She smiled at the bright-eyed creature as she closed and locked the cage, grabbed her jacket and purse off the back of the chair and headed for the door. "Thanks, Caruso. I needed that." Today of all days, she could use a little extra cheer in her life.

She'd lain awake half the night wondering where she and Mitch might find a middle ground—if there was one—on which they could try to rebuild some kind of relationship. The other half she'd spent trying to second-guess the confrontation she anticipated having with Grant Hahn and Arthur Lane this morning.

Sometime just before dawn, she'd realized that taking a stand sometimes meant that middle grounds and battlegrounds could become miserably synonymous.

Now, in the clear light of this late-November morning, things looked a bit brighter. At least the confrontation with her employer seemed unlikely, Cassie told herself as she weaved through the morning traffic on Speer Boulevard.

There was no picture accompanying the *Herald* article, this time. And even more importantly, as per her adamant instructions, Scott Avery had refrained from any mention of Hahn's department store. Grant Hahn—if he even saw the small article—would be hard-pressed to find anything in it that was even remotely connected to him.

In deference to Mitch's concerns—as well as her own—Cassie had reiterated to Scott Avery her need for anonymity. The reporter had been true to his word, but as she pulled into the garage behind Hahn's, the nagging certainty that her anonymity had long ago been compromised sent a familiar chill of fear slithering through her.

Forget what you saw, the message in the ruined displays had warned. And this morning, with her career, her personal future and perhaps even her very life hanging in the balance, Cassie wished with all her heart she could do just that.

Chapter Thirteen

Nothing could have prepared Cassie for what she encountered a scant five minutes later. Arthur Lane actually wore a smile as he motioned to her from across the sales floor.

Cassie acknowledged him with a tentative wave. Judging from the expression that lighted his long face, Cassie figured he either hadn't seen this morning's newspaper or someone had spiked his orange juice at breakfast.

"Ms. Craig." His greeting was more than genial as he caught up to her.

"Good morning, Arthur," Cassie responded cautiously.

"For some of us," he said, one eyebrow cocked knowingly. "Ms. Craig, would you be so good as to come with me to my office?" *Said the spider to the fly...* Cassie couldn't help adding to herself.

Since the first moment she'd met him, she hadn't trusted Arthur Lane, and this morning Cassie neither trusted nor understood his sudden display of polite good humor. "I've really got a lot to do today, Arthur," she said. "Can't it wait?"

"Oh, no, I'm afraid not," he said, shaking his head as he took her elbow, guiding her in the direction of his office. "This can't wait."

Cassie pulled her arm away from his grasp. "Well, all right, Arthur, if you say so," she relented. "But I hope this won't take too long."

He only smiled.

As they moved together toward the elevator, Cassie caught a glimpse of someone she recognized coming through the door. She stopped and watched the well-dressed young woman move across the sales floor and past the cosmetic counters.

"Suzanne?" Cassie called out. "Suzanne Leland?"

The dark-haired woman in the royal blue dress whirled around at the sound of her name and gave Cassie a curt nod. It was Suzanne, all right. But to Cassie's surprise, she didn't stop to speak, but instead, seemed to quicken her pace in the other direction toward the front of the store.

Cassie hadn't seen Suzanne since transferring from Metro State College to the New York design school where she had finished her degree. As she watched her former classmate and friend, Cassie remembered how they'd been in many of the same art classes and how they'd shared the same dreams of pursuing a career in fashion and design. She also remembered Suzanne being a very talented artist, but never unfriendly.

"You know Miss Leland?" Arthur asked.

"Yes," Cassie said thoughtfully as she watched Suzanne proceed toward the front of the store. Cassie's mind searched for a single reason why Suzanne would be stepping up into the display window. In the end, she could come up with only one, and it wasn't one she could accept.

"What's going on, Arthur?" Cassie demanded, scorching him with her accusing glare.

"Why, I'm sure I don't know what you mean?"

"Suzanne Leland. That's what I mean. What's she doing in my displays?"

Arthur crossed his arms tightly over his chest and sighed impatiently. "I'd hoped we could discuss this in a professional manner, but I should have known your penchant for histrionics would make that impossible."

"Cut the crap, Arthur!" Cassie stormed.

His small eyes narrowed. "All right." He relented. "Suzanne Leland has taken over your contract, Ms. Craig. Effective today." He delivered the blow with a self-satisfied smirk that sent anger rippling though her.

"You can't be serious?"

"Oh, I'm completely serious, Ms. Craig. Your letter of termination is waiting for you in my office. Now, if you'll just step this way."

"But I have a contract," Cassie said, disbelieving.

"*Had* a contract, Ms. Craig," he corrected. "And you were warned. This morning's paper gave us the grounds for your dismissal."

"But you can't do this!"

"I'm afraid we can and we have. Now, if you'll just follow me."

"Get out of my way, Arthur," Cassie warned him as she brushed past him toward the elevator. If Grant Hahn thought she'd fade conveniently into the woodwork merely on the orders of his assistant manager, he had another thing coming. If the second article had been anything like the first, Cassie might have understood her employer's reaction.

But it wasn't. She'd been painfully specific in her demands to Scott Avery and he'd listened. There was no picture, no mention of Hahn's, and, damn it, now there was just no reason for this unfair reaction from Grant, Cassie told herself.

Anger propelled her past the startled employees on the main floor and blinded her to their curious stares. Inside the elevator, Cassie's mind scrambled to find the words she'd use when she confronted Grant Hahn.

"Where is he?" she demanded as she burst into the executive offices and confronted a startled Ruth Palmer.

"He's not in." Ruth frowned, rose to her feet and came around the desk, positioning herself protectively between Cassie and the door that led into Grant's office.

"I don't believe you," Cassie blurted. "I want to see him, Ruth. It's important."

"See for yourself, Cassie." Ruth stepped aside.

Cassie opened the door and glanced into the empty office.

"He's not even in the building, Ms. Craig." The sound of Arthur's voice behind her sent a fresh wave of anger coursing through her. "Now if you'll just sign here..." He spread what she guessed were her walking papers out onto Ruth's desk.

"I'm not signing anything," Cassie snapped. "Ruth, is Mrs. Hahn in the building?"

Ruth and Arthur exchanged exasperated glances.

"Well, is she?" Cassie demanded.

"I'm sure I wouldn't know," Ruth sniffed, and moved back behind her desk and sat down.

"Really, Ms. Craig, it will do you no good to appeal to Lisa," Arthur said. "She doesn't have anything to do with the business end of things."

"Can I use this?" Cassie didn't wait for Ruth's answer, but reached for the phone and started dialing.

"Cassie, wait..." Ruth started to protest.

"Let her call anyone she pleases," Arthur put in smugly. "It won't do her any good."

How Cassie remembered the number for the Hahn residence, she'd never know, but her fingers punched out the numbers in rapid succession and, in a few moments, the voice of Estelle Hahn came on the line.

"Cassie, dear," Estelle said brightly. "What a nice surprise."

"Estelle, may I please speak to either Grant or Lisa?"

"I'm afraid neither is home at the moment."

Cassie glared at Arthur, who wore a satisfied smile, and the disappointment and frustration welling inside threatened to overwhelm and humiliate her.

"Cassie, are you still there?" Estelle asked. "Is something wrong, dear?"

"I've been fired," Cassie said, fighting to hold back angry tears. "Arthur Lane is standing here, right now, with my terminated contract."

Estelle gasped. "Oh, my dear! How terrible for you. Now let me think—there must be a way to rectify the situation. If only Grant were here..."

"I have to go now," Cassie said quickly. "Just tell Lisa or Grant that I'll be calling them again. Soon. I'm not taking this lying down, Estelle," Cassie warned, her voice cracking. "It just means too much."

"Of course it does, my dear," Estelle replied sympathetically. "I know this whole thing can be resolved. It's just a terrible misunderstanding, I'm sure."

"Well, I'm not so sure," Cassie muttered despondently.

"Everything will work out," Estelle insisted. "Your ideas for the displays were simply delightful. Now, don't you worry about a thing. And whatever you do, don't sign anything. Just go home. Calm down. Have a cup of tea. Don't do anything until you hear from me. I'll call just as soon as I can."

"All right," Cassie agreed reluctantly. Estelle's assurances had given her at least a meager thread of hope to cling to.

"I'm sure we can clear this whole matter up, and in a few short hours things will be right again. Now, put Arthur on the line, will you, dear?"

Cassie handed Arthur the phone and without looking back, she walked out of the executive offices and stepped into the elevator.

Once on the main floor, she headed straight to the exit. Blessedly, there was no one in the area to see the tears shimmering in her eyes as she rushed out of the store.

SHE HADN'T SEEN Mitch's car when she pulled up in front of her building, but she saw him waiting for her at the front entrance. She took a deep breath and glanced in the mirror before she got out of the car.

He smiled sympathetically as she walked toward him, and she read it in his eyes. He already knew she'd been fired.

"Who told you?" she asked as they walked upstairs to her apartment.

"Arlene."

"When did you talk to her?" she asked, fumbling for her keys.

"I called the store, hoping you'd let me take you to Jade Gardens for lunch," he explained. "I thought it would be a great place to begin our peace talks."

"Sorry, Dempsey. But somewhere shortly after I was fired, I lost my appetite," she explained as she pushed open the door and crossed over to the couch where she slumped down dejectedly.

"You were fired because of the follow-up article?"

She nodded. "Without a doubt, though I really didn't get much of an explanation," she said bitterly. "I tried to talk to Grant Hahn, but he wasn't in. Lisa wasn't available either, but I spoke with Estelle. She's pleading my case," Cassie said with a halfhearted smile.

"Do you think she can help?"

Cassie sighed and let her head drop back onto the cushions. "Oh, I don't know, Mitch. I get the idea her eccentricity is merely tolerated by her nephew and his wife. But as far as her role in the day-to-day operations of the store..."

"You never know, Cass. She *is* family. Maybe Grant will listen to what she has to say."

"I suppose you saw the article, as well?"

"I did," he said flatly.

"Well, let's have it. You might as well have your say, Dempsey, everyone else has."

Mitch shook his head. "I was wrong," he said evenly. "You had every right to make your own decision, Cass. I guess old habits are just not that easy to break."

"I know," she said softly. "Believe me."

He took her hand and squeezed it gently. "I'm sorry about your job, babe."

"I really wanted to make those displays a hit," Cassie said wistfully. "Did I tell you that I'd rigged it so that the lights would come on inside the display at the exact moment the Parade of Lights rounded the corner?"

He nodded. "I'm in love with a genius."

She looked at him and sighed. How did he always know just the right thing to say?

"Anyway, I hope they'll keep that part," she said. "It was a great idea. It really was." Her voice cracked, but she held her tears in check.

He handed her his handkerchief, but she waved it away.

"Damn it," she sputtered, jumping to her feet. "It could have been such a great Christmas."

"It still can be," he promised, putting his arms around her.

"Mitch . . ." she said, pulling reluctantly out of his embrace. "I need time. So much has happened."

For a moment, he only stared at her, seemingly lost in his own thoughts. Then, without warning, he turned

and walked into her bedroom. She followed him and
leaned against the door as he crossed over to the dresser
and opened her jewelry box. When he reached in and
pulled out the velvet ring box, her heart turned over.

"What do you think you're doing?" She tried to
sound irritated, but instead she only managed to sound
a bit breathless.

"It can still be a wonderful Christmas, Cass." He
held the ring box out to her, and she felt his gaze on her
face. She couldn't look at him, and the burning lump
swelling in her throat made speech impossible.

"Just think about it," he urged gently. "Try it on for
size. You might be surprised how good it feels."

"Damn it, Lisa, you've gone too far, this time,"
Grant declared vehemently as he walked around behind the bar and poured himself a drink. The small wet
bar in the corner of the plush South Denver hotel suite
wasn't nearly as well stocked as his own, but it'd do. He
wasn't a drinking man, but tonight he wanted a drink.
He *needed* a drink.

Throwing his head back, he swallowed; the pungent
amber liquid burned his throat and made his eyes water.

"How could I have known it would come to this?"
she whined.

He shook his head. "Come on, Lisa. What did you
think would happen?"

She plopped down onto the bed, her lips closed in a
stubborn pout. He studied her as he had at dinner,
taking in her big, round, cornflower blue eyes and her
flawless complexion. It wasn't just her youthful beauty

that held him in such a powerful grip, Grant told himself. He loved Brandon, loved the boy with all his heart, but it wasn't only the child. It was Lisa, herself. With all her weaknesses, he possessed an appetite and a passion for her that always left him hungry for more. Her vulnerability had always touched him. Her childlike charm intrigued him. And though her impulsiveness irritated him sometimes, her spontaneity fascinated him.

When he remembered how they used to be and what he'd dreamed they would become, he mourned for what they'd lost and grieved the future that seemed filled with only more pain.

Why then, he asked himself now, did he still believe that somehow, someday, everything would eventually work out? Especially now.

"Grant?" she prodded. "Can't you at least try to understand? You act as though I wanted all of this to happen."

"Oh, for God's sake, Lisa! Let me think." He slumped down into a chair and studied his drink. This woman, and his obsession with her, would be his ruin, he told himself with grim resignation.

When she moved up behind him and put her hands on his back, he leaned into her touch for a moment before abruptly jerking away. She swallowed his rejection and slumped down into a chair, facing him.

"Will you give him the money?" she asked simply. When he didn't answer, she asked him again.

"Don't I always pay your way?" he grumbled.

She didn't answer; she didn't have to. They both knew he had always paid and that he always would.

"I'm prepared to present him with the deal of a lifetime in exchange for his silence," he said evenly.

"There's ...still the matter of ...Cassie Craig," she reminded him tentatively.

"I know. I know," he muttered grimly before draining his glass. "What the hell did you hope to accomplish by trashing the displays, Lisa?" he demanded to know.

"I was trying to scare her off, don't you see? I thought maybe she'd drop the whole thing."

"Didn't you realize your card number would be recorded on the security system? What if she'd insisted we call the police, or contacted them on her own? Arthur even saw you leaving the store that morning. What if a custodian or other employee had seen you?"

She shook her head.

"Stupid, Lisa. Just plain stupid and dangerous."

"I guess I just didn't think," she muttered wearily.

"You never do," he said, his anger mounting. "It's lucky for you we can trust Arthur. When I caught him in his attempt to cover for you, he was unapologetic. He's half in love with you, you know."

Her humorless laugh was brittle. "One thing about old Arthur, he's loyal."

He shot her a withering glare. "That word doesn't hold much meaning for you, does it, Lisa?"

She lowered her eyes, finding it difficult to face the pain she knew her betrayals had put in his eyes. It hadn't always been this way, she thought miserably. In the early days, in Albuquerque, they'd had to struggle to keep their hungry eyes and eager hands off each other.

But in Denver everything had changed. His snooty friends, the miscarriage, Brandon's kidnapping, it had all been just too much for her to handle. Worst of all, she knew she'd disappointed him. Sometimes it was the disappointment and disapproval that were the hardest to bear. The pills and the booze were the only things that erased the pain, at least for a little while.

Day by day, the bonds of their marriage had been stretched beyond repair. Without a word, she knew Grant blamed her for all of it. His evenings at the store became more frequent, his return home later. Eventually he'd moved out of their bedroom.

And now, maybe he was right. Maybe this time she *had* gone too far.

"When does he want to meet?" Grant asked, interrupting Lisa's grim introspection.

"Tomorrow."

"Set it up," he said as he rose and headed for the door. His accusing glare scorched her. "Just tell me one thing, Lisa, and if you remember how, try telling the truth."

Lisa felt the knot of shame tightening in her stomach and for an instant, hated the man pulling the cords.

"Were you the one behind the wheel? Did you run that poor bastard down or didn't you?"

"I told you, I—I don't know," she stammered. "Sure, I'd had a few drinks but..."

"Don't you always?" His accusing stare was unwavering.

"I'd had a few drinks," she repeated, her voice rising defensively. "We argued. I wanted to drive. He says he tried to stop me."

"But you wouldn't listen."

"I don't remember," she said. "I don't remember!" she yelled again. "How many times do I have to tell you?"

She walked behind the bar and filled her glass. Tipping her head back, she took a long, deep swallow, willing the numbing liquid to blur her memory even more.

When he came up behind her and snatched the bottle from her hand, she swayed and nearly fell. Without warning, he hurled the bottle across the room. It exploded in a glittering shower of splintered glass and shimmering liquid against the wall above the bed.

She shrieked when he grabbed her arm and drew her to him, forcing her face within inches of his own.

"So help me, Lisa," he growled, "if this thing gets out... if it threatens the Crystal Creek project in any way..."

"The Crystal Creek project?" she cried. "Is that all you care about? A man is dead, Grant! A man is dead and I may have murdered him."

He let go of her and she slumped down onto the floor, sobbing.

"Did you hear what I said, you sanctimonious bastard?" she yelled up at him. "A man is dead! Run down outside your precious department store."

He reached out for her. "Damn you, Lisa," he whispered through clenched teeth, and then, letting his hand fall to his side, he turned his back on her. How could he want her and hate her so much at the same time?

"Stay here through the weekend," he ordered, his chilling calm incredibly restored. "I'll take of everything."

She struggled to her feet, staggered over to the bed and picked up the phone. "This is Mrs. Hahn in Room 513," she sniffed, glaring at him defiantly as he headed for the door.

"We've had a little accident. Send up a maid and another bottle of your best whiskey. And make it a big one," she added as her husband slammed out of the room.

THE MARKSMAN CROUCHED on the rooftop, hovering against the evening cold. He trained his binoculars on the target standing behind the glass across the street and drew a steadying breath. Luck was with him tonight.

For the past week she'd either been with her cop boyfriend or at work. Tonight, at last, she was alone. The opportunity was too good to miss.

He'd calculated his risks and knew the odds were in his favor. The weapon was an excellent choice for this distance, and due to the slight modifications he'd made, the noise would be minimized. His escape route was free of obstacles, the late-night street free of witnesses. He'd practiced and timed his retreat. He could do it in his sleep. His alibi—if he needed her—was waiting for him even now in his bed.

It shouldn't have come to this, he told himself at the last second, but now that it had, there was no turning back. Even if he'd been able to recover the keys, it wouldn't have made any difference. She was getting too close. She couldn't be allowed to come any closer to the truth. Too much was at stake. The risks were too high.

Raising the rifle to his shoulder, he centered the target at the vortex of the cross hairs. His finger lingered only a moment before he squeezed the trigger.

Chapter Fourteen

Cassie curled up on the couch and drifted into an uneasy sleep, waiting for Estelle to call. She didn't know how long she'd been sleeping, but the room was dark when the sudden sound of shattering glass startled her awake.

A chilling draft blew across the room. She wrapped the quilt around her and got to her feet, feeling momentarily disoriented by her sudden awakening. For the life of her, Cassie couldn't remember leaving the patio doors open, but the sheer curtains whipping frantically in the freezing air told her she must have.

She hurried to close the doors and, as her sleep-clouded mind cleared, she realized she hadn't left her doors open, after all. The doors were broken. Jagged shards of shimmering glass lined the frame like a row of crooked teeth. Broken glass was scattered everywhere. And something else was wrong. Dreadfully wrong.

"Samantha!" she gasped, blinking in disbelief at the mannequin, its headless silhouette outlined grotesquely by the glow of the streetlights below.

What on earth? Cassie's startled mind couldn't take it all in until she switched on a lamp and spotted the gaping hole in the wall above the couch where moments ago she'd been sleeping. Her knees trembled and she felt a sudden light-headedness as she moved to the phone. Her hands shook as she dialed 911.

"Yes, that's right," she repeated, her voice shaky and thin. "Someone shot through my window. Please send the police right away."

Cassie shuddered as she hung up the phone, and jumped when it rang while her hand was still on the receiver. She snatched it up and held it to her ear.

"Hello?" she said, barely recognizing her own voice that sounded strained, paper-thin and miles away.

"Cassie? What's wrong? Did I wake you?"

Had his voice ever sounded more welcome? Had hers ever been harder to find as the dreadful conclusion that felt like an iron band around her lungs forced itself into words.

"Mitch, I've called the police. Someone just tried to kill me."

"THAT'S IT," declared the detective, holding up the tweezers that gripped the slug he'd pried out of the wall. Two uniformed cops pushed Cassie's sofa back against the wall.

"Call me at home," Mitch ordered. "I don't care what time it is. I want to know the lab results as soon as you get them."

The detective nodded. "My guess is that it was a high-powered rifle, pretty common among hunters in this area."

A picture of the rifle hanging over Jordan Sloane's fireplace formed instantly in Cassie's mind and she shuddered.

"Better put some plastic over that until you can get that glass replaced, miss," the officer suggested, motioning to the shattered doors. "It's supposed to get even colder before morning."

"Thanks, we'll take care of it," Mitch said evenly as he ushered all three policemen out of the apartment.

"Was the gun over Jordan Sloane's fireplace a high-powered rifle?" Cassie asked almost before the door closed.

Mitch's dark brows drew together in a tight frown. "Yes, it was," he said flatly.

"Mitch, have you checked out Jordan's alibi for Sunday night?"

He nodded. "I talked with the bartender at the Goal Post. He said he remembered seeing Jordan, in uniform with a woman on his arm Sunday night," Mitch said.

"Then Lisa lied when she said she was home Sunday night," Cassie said.

"The bartender didn't positively identify the woman as Lisa Hahn. What are you getting at, Cass? Tell me."

"Oh, I don't know," she answered, running a shaky hand through her tousled hair. "I guess I'm just trying to place someone—anyone—connected to Cal Vantana at the scene of the hit and run." How else could they begin to solve the puzzle with so many pieces still missing?

"Well, so far Jordan's alibi seems to hold up, except, with the time of death still a question, at least in my mind, it leaves a lot of loose ends and a lot of time unaccounted for.''

"But why would Jordan Sloane want to kill Cal?" Cassie asked. She wrapped her arms around herself to suppress the shiver her ugly speculations caused to skitter through her.

"Why does anyone want to kill another human being? Greed? Jealousy? Maybe Cal knew something, had something that someone else wanted."

"The keys to the Silver Ghost?" Cassie asked.

"Maybe. Or maybe Cal was moving in on Jordan's territory."

"Lisa?"

He shrugged. "According to the gossip you overheard in the break room, Jordan's relationship with Lisa is a very profitable one for him. Maybe Cal was trying to catch his own gravy train."

Mitch rubbed the back of his neck and frowned. "I get the feeling Sloane is into this thing up to his eyebrows. I think I'll pay him another visit. Besides, I'd like to get a better look at that rifle."

"Tonight?" Cassie asked, surprised.

"This morning," Mitch corrected, placing both hands gently on her shoulders and turning her around to see the first light of morning reflecting pink and orange off the irregular silhouette of the Rockies in the distance above the city. "Right after I buy you a big breakfast."

Cassie tried to smile. At the moment, she could think of nothing more appealing than a fresh cup of hot coffee and distancing herself from the bullet hole in her wall.

"Just let me freshen up and change clothes. It's been a long night."

"While you're at it, pack a bag," he said firmly.

Cassie stared at him, her mind not fully comprehending.

"You're staying at my place," he said. "I'm not letting you out of my sight until we find out what the hell happened here tonight. No arguments."

"At the moment, I can't think of a single one," Cassie said wearily, staring at the bits of plaster and glass that littered her living room floor. "Get me out of here, Dempsey. But you can forget about breakfast, I think I've lost my appetite, again."

MITCH PULLED the Porsche up in front of the coffee shop and turned off the ignition. Cassie was out of the car and standing on the sidewalk before he could get around to open her door.

"I need coffee," she said wearily. "Badly. This has truly been the morning from hell."

"I know what you mean," he said, following her toward the entrance.

Had it only been a matter of hours since she'd listened to Caruso's sweet song and believed that everything might work out? "Caruso!" Cassie exclaimed, whirling around and almost crashing into Mitch.

She answered his questioning stare, "Lucille's canary," she explained as she hurried back toward the car. "I can't just leave him there, Mitch. With the glass broken, the apartment will be too cold for him. I've got to go back for him."

Ten minutes later, they pulled up outside Cassie's apartment building. "I'll be right back," she said reaching for the door handle.

"I'll go," he said. "Give me your keys."

Initially his authoritative tone made her bristle, but on second thought, she handed him the keys. The awful picture of the bullet hole in her wall and the gruesome sight of Samantha's head scattered all over the living room had already burned a permanent place in her memory. She decided she could use a few more hours before she had to face it again. "Thanks," she said softly.

She watched Mitch move quickly across the street. As usual, an appreciation for his athletic grace stirred inside her. Cassie leaned her head back against the seat and closed her tired eyes. Lack of sleep and tension had built into a dull throb behind her eyes.

After a few moments, she opened her eyes again and peered across the street. What was taking Mitch so long? she wondered. She waited another minute before deciding to go after him. Maybe he was having trouble maneuvering the cage and its stand through the hallway. At least she could open the front door for him when he came down.

But just as she stepped out of the car, Mitch emerged from the apartment building. He didn't have the bird cage, but carried a cardboard box, instead.

The grave expression shrouding his handsome features told her immediately that something was wrong. "Mitch?" she asked, meeting him on the sidewalk in front of the Porsche. "What's wrong?"

He shook his head. "Get back in the car, Cass," he said, his voice gruff.

Cassie was too concerned to challenge his order. "Where's Caruso?" she asked when they were seated inside the Porsche once more.

He turned and placed the small box in the back seat. "Caruso's dead," he said softly.

Guilt washed over her in a sickening wave. "Oh, no! I killed him!" Cassie cried miserably. "He couldn't take the cold. Oh, Mitch, I feel just awful. I shouldn't have left him. Poor Lucille. She trusted me to take care of him."

Mitch put his arm around her shoulders and stroked her arm. "It wasn't the cold, Cass," he assured her. "You didn't kill him."

"What? I don't understand. Mitch, where did you get that box? What's going on?" A horrified thought dawned. "Is Caruso inside that box?"

Mitch grabbed her hand as she reached into the back seat for the box. "Don't," he said firmly.

"Mitch? What is it? I have to know."

He stared at her a moment, unblinking, then slowly he reached for the box, set it between them and lifted the lid.

Cassie gasped as she stared down at the lifeless form inside, its small orange head appearing grossly oversize due to the white adhesive tape wound around its tiny beak.

"Caruso!" She choked. "Oh, my God, Mitch, who could have done such a horrible thing?"

"The driver," he said, his eyes sparking with unconcealed rage. "It's a warning, Cass. He knows his shot missed its mark. Caruso's death is another warning for you to keep silent.''

THEY DROVE BACK to the coffee shop in silence. Mitch went inside and bought coffee for both of them and brought it back outside in paper cups. Then he walked to the pay phone to call the lab.

While Mitch made his call, Cassie got out of the car and went into the rest room at the back of the coffee shop. She leaned over the cool porcelain sink and splashed cold water onto her face and ran a brush through her hair.

"Get a grip, Cassie," she whispered to herself as she stared into the mirror at her red-rimmed eyes.

Someone was trying to scare her away from the truth, and whoever it was had done a frighteningly good job. She was scared, all right. To the core. But somewhere deep inside her, something else besides fear began to stir. Something dark and seething. Anger. Red hot, indignant, outraged anger.

She'd been chased down an alley, lost her job, threatened, shot at and now chased away from her home. Bit by bit, the driver, or whoever was after her, was taking control of her life, and Cassie didn't like it, not one bit.

"Enough is enough," she vowed under her breath. She'd be damned if she'd lose any more without a fight.

Back out on the sidewalk, Cassie breathed deeply and welcomed the crisp morning air that seemed to somehow strengthen her new resolve.

"Feeling better?" Mitch asked as he opened her door and ushered her back inside the Porsche.

She felt the concern in his eyes and it touched her. "Much better. Now where's that coffee?"

Mitch smiled when he handed her a cup. As he walked around the front of the car, Cassie couldn't help casting a quick look into the back seat. The small cardboard box was gone, as somehow she knew it would be. It was so like him to try to protect her from any more pain. It was so like the old Mitch, the Mitch she remembered loving.

"Did the lab have any results yet?" she asked as he climbed into the driver's seat and closed his door.

"Nothing yet. I'd hoped to have enough to ask for a warrant to confiscate Sloane's rifle."

"What do we do now?" Cassie asked, her voice sounding stronger than it had all morning.

"Well, we could give Jordan Sloane a wake-up call, if you're feeling up to it."

"No time like the present." Cassie forced a small smile. "But, without a warrant, what can you do? I doubt he'll turn his rifle over to you willingly."

"I won't even ask. But if I can get a closer look, a better description of the gun, maybe even a model number, it might speed up a warrant, if and when the lab boys make their determination."

In less than ten minutes, they were turning onto the quiet residential street where Jordan Sloane lived.

"Look! There he is," Cassie exclaimed.

Mitch pulled up to the curb several houses away and let the Porsche idle. Together they watched as Jordan tossed something into the trunk of the long, black limousine parked in the driveway.

Cassie gasped. "Was that what I think it was?"

"A gun case," Mitch growled. "I'd bet a month's pay that case contains a very hot, very incriminating rifle."

Panic seized Cassie as she watched Jordan back the sleek limo out of the driveway. "Mitch, do something! He's getting away!"

"Patience, my sweet," Mitch admonished as he pulled back out onto the street. "We'll just follow our nervous chauffeur and see what he intends to do with his cargo."

Patience was something Cassie was running short of this morning. Maybe it was the coffee, or the gunshot that had shattered her life in a dozen directions, or the jarring picture of the headless Samantha that kept forming in her mind every time she closed her eyes.

"You'd better step on it, Dempsey," she urged him, distressed by the distance she saw growing between them and the Hahn limousine. "What if we lose him and he ditches the gun and we never find it?"

"We won't lose him," he assured her, and reached over and squeezed her hand lovingly. "He's driving a very recognizable vehicle. And if we should lose sight of him, I'll call in the troops." He nodded at the car phone. "He won't be hard to spot."

Cassie felt a little better, but she still strained her eyes to see the dark limo in the traffic ahead of them. When she saw the flashing signal, she said, "He's turning onto Sixth, Mitch."

"I see him," he assured her as he changed lanes to follow.

In a few more minutes, they passed the large homes that bordered the exclusive Crystal Creek area, and Jordan Sloane's destination became clear. He was on his way to the Hahn mansion.

"It'll be hard to stay out of sight on the two lane road," Cassie explained.

"As I remember, there are a lot of secluded private roads up there," Mitch recalled. "We'll get as close as we can, and then turn onto one of them and walk the rest of the way."

"Why do I get the sinking feeling that I should have shoved some dog biscuits into my pocket?"

Mitch flashed her a ready smile. "No way," he assured her. "Our 'Mission Impossible' days are behind us. I only want to get close enough to see what goes on when he gets to the mansion. If he tries to ditch the gun on the way, we'll catch him in the act."

The limo kicked up dust and rocks as it sped around the winding curves. Sloane showed no sign of stopping. When they were within a quarter of a mile of the entrance to the Hahn property, Cassie told Mitch they'd better stop to avoid overtaking the limo when Sloane slowed down to turn into the drive.

At the next private road, Mitch pulled over and guided the Porsche carefully off the shoulder and into the scrub oak. Cassie heard the bushes scraping against the sides of the car and winced as she visualized deep scratches in the perfect paint job.

"Anything for the cause," Mitch muttered miserably.

In a few moments, as they jogged back toward the main road, Cassie remembered the wooded lot that bordered the Hahn property.

"This way," she said, heading off in a diagonal line through the trees. Beyond the pines, they spied the rolling grounds that surrounded the three-story stone residence. Moving closer, they positioned themselves at the edge of the trees, about a hundred yards away and facing the front of the mansion.

"There he is," she whispered as the limousine pulled up in the semicirclular driveway. They watched Jordan get out of the car and jog up the steps to the front door. The door opened, but because of their distance from the house and the angle of the morning sun that cast the porch in deep shadow, Cassie and Mitch couldn't see who answered the door.

"What now?" Cassie asked.

"We wait. He might come back for the gun."

"I never knew police work could be so boring," Cassie complained after ten minutes.

He smiled and touched a shimmering lock of chestnut brown that had fallen onto her forehead. The intimate gesture caused a familiar flutter in her chest. She returned his smile and touched his hand, which lingered on her cheek. A gentle warmth flowed between them despite the bite of winter in the morning air.

The sound of a car door closing jerked their attention back to the subject of their surveillance.

"He's leaving!" Cassie cried.

"Come on," Mitch called out as they jogged through the woods back to the Porsche. "We can wait for him on the side road and follow him back into town."

A few moments later, they saw the limo speed by, kicking up rocks as it raced down the road in a cloud of dust.

"He acts as though the devil himself were on his tail." Mitch stepped down on the accelerator and pulled the Porsche back out onto the main road.

"Do you think he saw us?"

"There's little chance of that. He's stirring up so much dust he probably wouldn't see us if we were right behind him. Look at that idiot!" Mitch said as they rounded the next curve in time to see the end of the limo fishtail across the narrow road and then whip back violently across the soft shoulder.

"Mitch, you'd better slow down," Cassie cautioned. "I don't see how he can keep making these curves the way he's driving."

Mitch eased off the accelerator as they cruised into the next turn and were immediately enveloped in a blinding cloud of dust.

"Look out!" Cassie screamed as she saw glossy black and chrome looming right in front of them. Mitch cranked the wheel hard to the left and barely missed smashing into the back end of the limo, which had skidded into an ancient blue spruce at the side of the road.

As soon as the Porsche skidded to a stop, Mitch jumped out of the car and raced over to the limousine.

Cassie was right behind him. As she moved up beside Mitch, she saw Jordan Sloane's inert form slumped over the steering wheel. A steady flood of crimson poured from the ugly gash above his eye.

"Get on the phone, Cass," Mitch ordered as he jerked open the driver's-side door of the limo.

Cassie nodded and dragged her eyes away from the blue athletic jacket and the black ball cap lying on the back seat of the limo. It took her a few seconds to figure out the buttons and switches on the car phone, but in less than a minute, a Denver Police Department dispatcher was on the other end assuring Cassie that help was on the way.

"Please hurry," Cassie urged into the receiver before she hung up and rushed back to the limousine to see if she could help in any way.

But one look at Mitch's face told her there was nothing she could do. No matter how fast help arrived, it would be too late to help Jordan Sloane.

Chapter Fifteen

The ride across town had been a quiet one. Cassie didn't feel like talking. Numbed and dazed, she felt like a powerless participant in the bizarre events that seemed to twist and turn out of control at every corner.

Looking back, it felt as though she'd been a sleepwalker moving through an incomprehensible nightmare ever since the night of the hit and run that had taken Cal Vantana's life. Could she dare believe it was really over?

The ball cap and jacket in the back seat of the limo confirmed, at least in Cassie's mind, that Jordan Sloane had been her burglar. Mitch assured her, after examining the weapon, that the rifle in the trunk would match the bullet in Cassie's wall. The evidence was there, Cassie told herself. Why then, couldn't she believe the nightmare was over?

It was almost noon before Mitch pulled into the driveway of his neat southwest Denver ranch-style home. He carried her bag as Cassie followed him up the walk. Once inside, she felt the mental curtain she'd drawn at the scene of Jordan Sloane's death lifting.

Almost immediately the tangible reminders of her life with Mitch reached out to greet her. Bittersweet memories churned as she caught a glimpse of herself in the mirror of the large oak coat tree just inside the door. Cassie studied her tired reflection briefly, remembering how Mitch had proudly declared the coat tree an antique that spring afternoon when he'd dragged it home from the flea market.

In the living room, she spied the old upright piano that they'd refurbished together. She closed her eyes, and for a moment, she could almost hear the gentle strains of the song he'd played for her that snowy Christmas eve.

Blinking back that emotionally charged memory, Cassie's eyes drifted to the far end of the room. An enlarged photograph of a stand of lacy aspen trees with snowcapped peaks in the background held a prominent place over the native stone fireplace. Cassie remembered the golden autumn afternoon in Telluride when she'd snapped the picture.

"Make yourself at home," Mitch said, interrupting her reverie. "The bathroom's down the hall. The bedroom's in here."

"The couch will be fine," she said quietly, following him as he walked into the bedroom with her bag. "Really," she insisted. "I'll only be here until the landlord can replace the glass doors. I don't want to put you out, Mitch."

He dropped her bag onto the bed and turned around to face her. "Then don't," he said flatly, moving up close enough to touch. "The bed is king-size. And as I remember, in the old days we had plenty of room in a bed half this size.''

His sensual gaze held her for a moment where she stood. Like an invisible touch, it caressed her. "You remember a lot about the old days, don't you, Mitch?''

"I do," he said, his voice husky as he reached out for her. "There were some good times, weren't there? Times I don't ever want to forget. Don't you remember, Cass?''

He felt her stiffen in his arms as she fought the effects of his embrace. "You forced me to forget. You seem to have forgotten that you didn't give me much choice.''

The bitterness of her words felt like a sharp jab to his gut, and he released her. When he stepped back and looked into her eyes, he could see with painful clarity two years' emptiness staring back at him.

She was right, he admitted to himself. He had no right, no right at all to ask her for another chance. Maybe it was time he accepted the fact that he'd lost her.

"I expect the lab to call later tonight," he said, averting his gaze from her face and forcing the businesslike and professional tone that ten years as a cop had taught him—about as far from what he was feeling as New York was from Denver, about as far as Cassie was from him now. The renewed sense of loss made him feel gutted.

"I have no doubt Sloane's rifle and the slug they dug out of your wall will be a match. You'd better get some rest. They'll want a formal statement later,'' he explained as he turned and walked out of the room, closing the door behind him.

When he heard the sound of the door opening, he turned and saw her leaning against the door staring at him.

"Cassie? Is there something else?"

She nodded. Her eyes shimmered a priceless emerald green. "Those good times, Mitch," she said softly, "I was just trying to remember them. And I was thinking . . . maybe you could give me a little help?"

In a heartbeat he closed the space between them and gathered her into his arms. His mouth came down on hers with a passion that rocked them both. When she felt him scoop her up off the floor and move into the bedroom, she buried her face in his neck and inhaled his familiar clean, male scent.

Closing her eyes, Cassie let the memories flow, overwhelming her with their intensity. "I can't make any promises," she said, her voice husky with emotion.

"You don't have to," he said as he carried her to the bed, kicking the door closed behind them on the way. "You don't have to say another word."

THREE HOURS LATER, nestled against the muscular length of him, Cassie listened to the sound of his deep velvet voice fill the evening air.

"The night Brian died," he began softly, "I thought it was the end of the world. Watching Holly, his kids and his family—seeing all that pain—somehow everything got all twisted around. Instead of grabbing the one thing in the world that would have made it all bearable, I forced you away from me."

When she snuggled closer, he stroked her cheek and kissed the top of her head.

He sighed. "I was a fool to shut you out. Without telling you why, I tore us apart. I was wrong," he said hoarsely. "Dead wrong. All I could think about was the risk you'd be taking if you promised to spend your life with Mitch Dempsey, the cop, the next target for some wacko with a gun. I was wrong to make that decision for us. But believe me, Cass, I never doubted for one moment that you'd be the best wife—the best partner any man could hope to have."

She rose up on one elbow. "And now?" she asked as her gaze searched and found the clear blue light of truth in his eyes.

His hand moved tenderly to the base of her neck and drew her face down slowly to meet his. He kissed her deeply, desperately, his lips answering her question in a way his words could never have expressed. He ignited the passion inside her and it exploded once more in a frenzy of desire and urgency.

"Mitch," she whispered when he lifted his lips from her mouth. "I think I remember everything now."

He smiled and kissed her again. "I want to marry you, Cass," he said. "Marry me, and we'll spend this Christmas and the rest of our lives celebrating."

His promises wrapped themselves around her heart like satin ribbons. "But so much has happened," she said, falling back onto the pillow. *You need time to sort it all out,* her common sense whispered. *Time to get back to your real life. Time alone to think.* "I need time," she whispered hoarsely, her eyes closed.

He felt his heart constricting painfully inside him. "I thought being together again made you happy."

She nodded. *Happy* wasn't the word. The past few hours of rediscovery had been pure joy. "The original idea was that I stay here for protection, remember? Now that we know it was Jordan Sloane who tried to kill me, we also know it was Jordan who must have killed poor Cal. I don't need protecting anymore, Detective Dempsey," she declared. "What I need now is time and space away from you... away from this wonderful king-size bed to think things through."

He groaned and pulled her over on top of him. "Okay, so I can't protect you anymore, but while you're away doing all this thinking, just don't forget how much I love you, Cassie Craig."

She planted a kiss on his forehead and then, reaching for his hand, brought it to her mouth and kissed each finger seductively. "It's a deal," she said, smiling. "But just make sure you keep reminding me how much."

IT HAD ONLY BEEN thirty-six hours since Cassie had gone back to her apartment, and Mitch had gone back to work. But the irony of their situation had struck him full force from the first hour away from her. Dropping down into his swivel chair, Mitch glanced up at the clock on the wall across the room. Six-fifteen.

"Time," he grumbled. It had become his worst enemy. She'd said she needed more time just when he'd decided they hadn't a moment to lose. Seeing even a flicker of uncertainty in her eyes, hearing any hint of doubt in her voice hurt him deeply. With a stab of guilt, he reminded himself that Cassie had endured that same kind of pain for the past two years.

He sighed and leaned back in his chair. It seemed the future he couldn't wait to get started would just have to wait a little longer. He owed her that much.

Mitch turned his attention back to the stack of files he'd been slogging through since his return to the office on Thursday. He hadn't finished as much as he would have liked this afternoon, and now he realized he'd have to take a stack home with him to finish over the weekend. So be it. He was used to working overtime. He'd work through the weekend gladly, but there was just no way he was working late tonight. He had a date and it was one he had no intention of breaking.

"Professional curiosity," she'd called it when she'd informed him of her intention to position herself outside of Hahn's when the Parade of Lights passed by. She wanted to be the first, she said, to see what her competitor had done with the displays.

"Masochistic," he'd called it. But Cassie, being her delightfully determined and solidly stubborn self, hadn't budged. Eight o'clock sharp, in front of Hahn's, she intended to be there with or without him. Finally they'd arranged that he pick her up at seven-fifteen.

By six-thirty, Mitch had reduced the stack on his desk to four files. He slapped the last one closed, figuring he could shower and change in the patrolman's locker room and still make it to Cassie's apartment in less than thirty minutes. He'd have liked nothing more than to surprise her by being early, but tonight he'd have to settle for merely being on time.

Mitch was halfway down the hall when he heard his phone. He ran back to his office and grabbed it on the second ring. "Dempsey," he barked.

"It's Jerry from the lab. I've got something here I thought you might want to see."

"Hey, look, Jerry," Mitch said, leaning one hip against the corner of the desk, "I was just on my way out. Can't it wait until Monday?"

"Sure, if you're in a hurry. I'll just file it."

"Thanks, I'll check in with you first thing Monday morning."

"I won't be in early," Jerry explained. "I'm pulling the weekend shift. But just tell the boys on duty Monday morning that you want to take a look at the Sloane report."

Mitch drew a quick, sharp breath. "Sloane? Jordan Sloane?"

"Yeah, I knew this was your case and I wanted to make sure you saw this report."

"Right, but I received that report yesterday, Jerry. The rifle was positively matched with the slug taken from the wall at Ms. Craig's apartment."

"This report doesn't have anything to do with the weapon," Jerry said. "It's the final autopsy report. I thought you might want to see it. Seems as if the car crash might not have been what killed Sloane, after all."

"But I was there. I saw the damage done when Sloane hit the dash. He was dead before the para-medic arrived."

"Right, right." Mitch heard the shuffling of paper and knew that when Jerry started talking again, he was paraphrasing from the coroner's report. "A severe blow to the head causing massive hemorrhaging resulting in death. That was their initial supposition, but after they studied the results of the tissue samples, they wrote an addendum. Looks like your boy got himself drugged. He was pumped so full of downers there was no way he could have known what hit him when he plowed into that tree."

"I'll be right down," came Mitch's curt reply.

He felt the pulse at his temples drum as he took the stairs two at a time down to the lab. The startling possibility that Jordan Sloane could have been murdered set a whirlpool of deadly questions and disturbing answers swirling in Mitch's mind.

Jordan Sloane was responsible for Cal Vantana's death, of that Mitch was deadly certain. But if Jordan Sloane had been murdered, did that mean he hadn't acted alone in his crime? The possibility had always been there, but suddenly it sent a chill of dread straight to the center of Mitch's heart.

If Jordan Sloane had been murdered, a desperate and cold-blooded murderer was still out there. And Cassie was still in grave danger.

CASSIE LET THE PHONE RING ten times before she gave up. She'd already waited fifteen minutes, nearly twenty. Why couldn't Mitch ever be on time? she asked herself irritably. Shoving aside her disappointment, she put on her coat and headed for the door.

She refused to be late. If Suzanne Leland had kept her idea of having the lights in the window coincide with the holiday parade, Cassie wanted to be there to at least have the satisfaction of seeing them go on.

The festive holiday crowds always gathered early for the opening night of the annual holiday parade and it would be impossible to find a place to park if she waited any longer. With or without Mitch, Cassie had no intention of being anywhere but smack-dab in front of Hahn's when the parade passed by.

Assuring herself that he knew where she'd be and at what time, she started out the door, digging through the bottomless pit of her leather bag for her car keys. The sound of the ringing telephone pulled her back inside.

Snatching up the receiver, she smiled to herself. "You're late, Dempsey," she declared.

For a moment there was an uncertain silence on the line.

"Mitch?"

"Cassie? Is that you?" The unfamiliar female voice sounded confused.

"This is Cassie," she said quickly, feeling foolish for her impetuous assumption that it had been Mitch calling.

"Cassie, this is Ruth Palmer."

Cassie was shocked. "Ruth? Well, I never expected to hear from you again," she responded frankly. Considering Ruth's unyielding loyalty to the firm and, more importantly, to her boss, Cassie was very surprised, indeed.

"I've got to talk to you, Cassie," Ruth said, her voice taking on an urgent edge. "It's vital."

"What is it, Ruth?" Cassie asked. "Is it something about the displays? Has something gone wrong?" A flicker of perverse pleasure flamed inside her. Maybe Suzanne hadn't been able to complete the windows in time and in desperation Grant Hahn had been forced to call Cassie back to finish the job and save the day.

Fat chance, Cassie told herself. Arthur Lane would pose as the nutcracker himself before he'd let Cassie set foot in Hahn's again. The thought presented an amusing image, and Cassie smiled despite herself.

"It's about the...the accident," Ruth said uncertainly, obliterating Cassie's smile along with any remnants of her vengeful fantasy.

"What accident? Ruth, what are you talking about?"

"The hit and run," Ruth said, her voice strained.

A knot of apprehension tightened in Cassie's stomach.

"I know who did it," she whispered desperately. "It wasn't Jordan Sloane behind the wheel and I can prove it."

Cassie stifled the gasp that set her heart racing. "What do you mean? Ruth, do you know what you're saying?" Cassie felt the blood drain from her face.

"I have proof. But I can't talk anymore," Ruth said. "Meet me in the executive offices in fifteen minutes. You still have your security card, haven't you?"

Arthur Lane's curt message left on her answering machine a couple of days ago ordering her to return her card came back to Cassie in a flash of remembrance.

It had been the day of the shooting, and with everything that had happened since, she had completely forgotten about the call, as well as the card she still carried in her wallet.

"Yes," Cassie said tentatively. "I still have it. But, Ruth, can't you just tell me what this is all about?"

"I have to go," Ruth said, sounding more desperate and agitated by the moment. "Just come. Please. Hurry. And bring the keys with you," she demanded. "The ones you found the night of the hit and run. I know you still have them. Bring them with you," she urged. "And hurry." Cassie was still clutching the receiver when the line went dead.

Chapter Sixteen

Inserting the security card into the electronic slot made Cassie feel like a criminal. She wondered if she was breaking the law as she stepped inside the dimly lit store and heard the door close and lock electronically behind her.

The store had closed at six; Cassie remembered that the later closing time of nine, adjusted for the holiday shopping, wouldn't begin until tomorrow.

As she made her way to the elevator, a shiver of nervous dread tickled down her spine. What could Ruth Palmer possibly have to show her? What proof had she uncovered and how did she know about the keys?

Cassie remembered Scott Avery's second article. There had been no mention of the keys in that story. Her mind whirled as gleaming metal doors whooshed open and she stepped inside. The elevator glided upward toward the executive offices, and Cassie's stomach did a violent drop and roll.

A terrifying thought struck her. If Jordan Sloane hadn't been the hit-and-run driver, then whoever had tried to silence her was still out there. Dear God, what if it was Ruth Palmer?

A rush of panic hit her at the precise moment the sound of the elevator bell announced her arrival on the executive floor. As her footsteps echoed through the deserted hallway, Cassie became chillingly aware of how alone she was. If only she'd tried to reach Mitch again before she'd left her apartment.

"Don't panic," she ordered herself in a breathless whisper. There was nothing to be afraid of. Why, the mere suggestion that Ruth Palmer could have been an accomplice to murder was absurd. What harm could come from merely listening to what she had to say? Besides, Cassie reminded herself, trying desperately to bolster her sagging courage, there was no reason to believe that the evidence Ruth claimed to have uncovered was legitimate. Until proven otherwise, Cassie would just have to believe that Jordan Sloane had been the hit-and-run driver.

In another moment, the door to the executive offices loomed before her. Taking a shaky breath, Cassie grasped the knob and turned it. The knob turned freely, but the door wouldn't open. It moved only a scant inch when she shoved against it, something inside seemed to be blocking it from opening all the way.

"Ruth?" Cassie called out nervously.

Silence.

Though the soft white light from the lamp sitting on Ruth's desk filtered out of the office, Cassie couldn't get the door open wide enough to see anything else.

"Ruth," she called out again, louder. "Are you in there? It's me, Cassie."

Cassie heard a rustling sound, and the door moved another inch. With a final shove, Cassie managed to open the door wide enough to allow her to slip inside.

Her hands flew to her mouth, and she gasped when she looked down at what—who—had been blocking the doorway.

"Oh, my God! Ruth!" Cassie cried as she dropped to her knees and bent over the lifeless form of the woman lying just behind the door.

"EXACTLY WHAT KIND of drug was it, Jerry?" Mitch asked without looking up from the coroner's report.

"Don't let its long medical name throw you, it's just a common prescription tranquilizer. Perfectly harmless when taken in the correct doses under doctor's orders, but a lethal weapon when mixed with alcohol or certain other drugs."

Mitch remembered Cassie telling him how Lisa had undergone treatment for her addictions. Had tranquilizers been one of them? "According to this report, Sloane ingested a huge amount of the stuff."

Jerry nodded. "Our investigation into Sloane's background didn't turn up any recent prescriptions. In fact, the guy hardly ever saw a doctor. It seems he was the picture of health."

"Yeah, except he wound up dead," Mitch said grimly. "When do they estimate he took the pills?" he asked, leafing impatiently to the end of the thick report.

"When factored in to the alcohol level, the medical examiner estimated Sloane couldn't have had more than a ten-minute head start on the toxic bomb ticking inside him.''

''Are you saying he was drunk?'' Mitch was surprised. If Jordan Sloane had been under the influence of anything the morning of his death, his driving on the way out to the Hahn residence certainly hadn't shown it.

''No way. Not even close,'' Jerry said, shaking his head. ''But with the large dose of tranquilizers found in his system, it only took a small amount of alcohol—a drink, even a fairly light one—to trigger the chemical reaction that sent him off the road and into that tree in a blind stupor.''

Mitch thanked Jerry for his help and jogged back upstairs to his office. After a quick call to Chief Anderson to update him on the coroner's report and to request a warrant from the D.A.'s office to search the Hahn residence, he punched in Cassie's number. He swore when she didn't answer.

He swore again when he glanced down at his watch. She'd left without him, so damn determined to be the first to get a look at those blasted displays. No doubt the entire Hahn clan would be gathered to view the unveiling, as well.

A few minutes later, stuck in the snarl of downtown traffic, Mitch's heart sank when he realized there was no way he could stop her, no way he could protect her now.

Maybe he was wrong. Maybe the conclusion he'd drawn was way off base. He hoped and prayed that he was. Because if he was right —as his gut told him he was—Cassie was headed for a rendezvous with a murderer.

"DON'T TURN AROUND," came the whispered order behind her. "I have a gun and I'd love an excuse to use it."

Cassie's heart and mind froze. "Who is it?" she asked, without moving a muscle. "What do you want? What have you done to poor Ruth?"

"Tsk-tsk," the voice scolded. "Always so full of questions."

Cassie felt the hard steel of the gun barrel press against the base of her neck.

"Stand up," the voice ordered. "Slowly. Move over to the desk."

Somehow Cassie's legs found the strength to obey. "Who are you?" she demanded, her voice trembling.

"Someone who's always had the Hahn family's best interests at heart, Cassie. And if you had, too, then Ruth Palmer would still be alive."

The taunting words sent a new shock of terror quivering through Cassie's already startled senses.

"But why? Why did you hurt poor Ruth?"

"Me? Why, I haven't done a thing," the whisper replied innocently.

Every nerve strained to recognize the voice behind her, but the voice was so low and raspy it was unrecognizable.

"But you killed her," Cassie cried in a shuddery whisper.

"Oh, Cassie, you do jump to the worst conclusions." The whisper mocked her. "When Ruth came in and found you, the disgruntled ex-employee rifling through her desk, she pulled the gun from her purse—she always carried it with her, you didn't know that, did you? Anyway, Ruth tried to stop you. But you overpowered her, struck her down, but not before she managed to get off a last deadly shot."

Cassie's knees felt weak. Her stomach churned. "What do you want from me?"

"The keys," the voice growled. "Where are they?"

Cassie heard an edge of desperation in the voice and knew instinctively that she had a bargaining chip. With courage she didn't know she possessed, Cassie whirled around to face her captor.

The grotesque mockery of the fully bearded, red-suited Santa holding her at gunpoint made Cassie's breath catch in her throat and her lungs burn. The padded red suit, along with the full white beard, bushy fake eyebrows and white shoulder-length hair successfully obscured the gunman's identity.

"What the . . . ?"

"Clever, isn't it? A department store Santa would hardly draw attention to himself as he slipped away in the holiday crowd, now would he?"

Cassie shook her head in stunned disbelief. Desperately she tried to shake off the shock that threatened to render her helpless.

"Give me the keys," the voice ordered.

Cassie unconsciously tightened the grip on her purse and stepped backward. Her eyes darted to the lamp on the edge of the desk, and a glimmer of hope sparked inside her. If she could get to it, the heavy brass lamp could become a weapon.

"The keys are in your purse, aren't they?"

Cassie nodded numbly, and though she could barely see her captor's eyes through the thick white hair, she knew they gleamed with victory.

"Hand them over," the whisper demanded.

Cassie made a great issue of pawing through her large leather bag, stalling for time.

"Find them, or I'll find them myself after you're dead."

"I'm trying," Cassie shot back, feigning courage despite the terror that welled inside her at the sight of the blue-black gun barrel pointed at her heart.

"Just tell me why," Cassie pleaded as she continued to dig through her purse and inch closer to the lamp. "Why did you do it?"

The Santa seemed taken aback by her question. "Isn't it obvious?"

Cassie shook her head.

"Because he had to be protected, of course. From all of them. He was going to adopt that child. That little cur pup of Lisa's. Don't you see? I had to step in. I couldn't let something like that happen."

Cassie's thoughts whirled; she stared at her captor, disbelieving. Was the gunman referring to the kidnapping of Lisa's son?

"Brandon?"

"Yes, little Brandon. But that fool Vantana didn't have the nerve to finish the job. He couldn't kill the kid, but he didn't have any trouble grabbing his share of the ransom money, did he? It should have lasted him for the rest of his miserable life, but when he came back and tried to blackmail me, it was his last mistake. Of course, I had to have him killed," the voice stated matter-of-factly, rising above a whisper for the first time.

Cassie's eyes widened in startled recognition, and her legs felt as though they would no longer support her. Dazed, she dropped down into the chair behind the desk.

A small smile moved the beard. "So you know who I am?"

Stunned, Cassie could only nod in shocked disbelief.

"Well, so be it. You might as well know the rest. You won't be taking my secrets anywhere but to the grave, will you, Cassie? Jordan Sloane was easy to manipulate," the gunman bragged. "With the generous offer to help his acting career along, he set it all up—the hit and run and disposing of Vantana's body. But he was as big a fool as Vantana," Cassie's captor sneered. "Trying to milk his little escapade for more money by blackmailing Lisa was his greatest mistake. It was easy to kill him," her captor boasted. "Lisa is so careless with her pills. And now, with Jordan out of the way, and Lisa scared silent, I only have you left to deal with."

"B-but the keys?" Cassie stammered. "What about the keys?"

"Ah, that vital piece of evidence connected to the kidnapping, but never found," the gunman mused. "Brandon had been fussy that night—he never was a very good baby. I gave him the keys to play with, to shut the brat up moments before I unlocked the door and let Cal into the mansion. The keys were still curled in his wretched little fist when Cal took him out of the house. I haven't laid eyes on them since."

Cassie was rocked as the details of Cal Vantana and his accomplice's crimes were revealed. "He kept them all these years," Cassie muttered softly. "Planning to come back someday and blackmail you."

"The Silver Ghost," her captor said wistfully. "It was always such a beautiful car. Grant gave me that gold charm attached to my very own set of keys for my birthday that year."

Cassie stood slowly, the blood pulsing in her ears. The gunman seemed temporarily lost in the past, unaware of Cassie's cautious movements. It was now or never, she told herself as she grabbed the heavy brass lamp and hurled it with all her strength at her captor.

The gun-wielding Santa shrieked and stumbled backward. The lamp crashed to the floor and went out, plunging the room in darkness. Cassie groped her way past Ruth's body to the door, suppressing the wave of nausea that would hinder her escape.

Out in the hall, she ran blindly for the red-lighted exit sign above the door to the stairwell.

Grasping the cold metal handle, she flung the door open and started a dizzying race to the main floor. A race for her life.

A few moments later, Cassie heard angry footsteps pounding after her. When she reached the landing on the third floor, the gunman shouted for her to stop and punctuated the command with shots.

Cassie screamed when she heard the bullets whizzing past her. The sound of the gunshots mingled with the sounds of her own terror exploded deafeningly, echoing and ricocheting through the narrow stairwell.

Fighting the hysteria that threatened to immobilize her, Cassie kept running, taking the stairs two at a time until she reached the main floor.

Disaster struck on the last stair. The pain was searing. It took her breath away when her foot slipped and her ankle twisted.

Desperately Cassie struggled to her feet, jerked open the door and limped out into the lingerie department. Tears of pain stung her eyes as she limped across the dimly lit first floor toward the employee exit.

Halfway there, she stopped. Panic seized her. She'd left her purse in Ruth's office, she realized with horror. The security card that would let her out of the building was in the wallet tucked safely inside her purse.

Suddenly she heard the stairway door open. Her stalker was now on the main floor with her. Dropping to her knees, Cassie crawled behind the nearest counter and crouched low.

Cassie spied the phone sitting beside the cash register and a spark of hope flared inside her. But that brief flame was instantly extinguished when she remembered the only phone with an outside line after-hours was the one at the back of the store at the employee exit. The one she'd used to call for help the night Cal Vantana had been murdered.

Cassie shirked away from that grisly thought, realizing she'd have to keep her wits and her emotions in check if she hoped to survive the nightmare that had sprung to life before her disbelieving eyes.

Despite her swelling, throbbing ankle, she had to get to that phone, Cassie told herself. Heart pounding, she began to edge her way around the counter. Every movement sent a fresh shock of pain through her leg.

Cassie scanned the main floor. Though she couldn't spot the gunman, she knew that deadly danger still surrounded her. She had to keep moving. It was only a matter of time before the murdering Santa found her.

Crouching low, Cassie began to edge her way painfully toward the next counter. When she heard a rustling movement ahead of her, she thought her heart would burst. The gunman was very near. Every instinct warned of the peril.

She dared not make a single move that would reveal her position. The thundering sound of Cassie's own heart hammering wildly against her chest was the only sound.

After a few agonizing moments, Cassie told herself she had to try again to get to the phone. But had her stalker moved closer? She held her breath and peered cautiously from behind the counter. The deranged Santa stood a mere six feet away from her hiding place. Cassie's heart sank.

To reach the phone at the employee exit, she would have to get past the gunman, but that would be impossible.

With her ankle becoming more immobilized by the minute, Cassie knew she'd never make it. The store, though dimly lighted, was far from dark enough to cover her movements. And even on two good legs, the distance was too far, too wide open, the menace that waited for her too deadly.

A raspy chuckle gurgled out from behind the beard as if the gunman had read her grim thoughts. "You can't escape, Cassie. Come out, come out, wherever you are," the voice taunted.

At that moment, Cassie heard another sound, the faint strains of music. A brass band! The parade was approaching, she told herself, and judging by the steady increase in the volume of the bright holiday melody, in a few minutes it would be directly in front of Hahn's.

Her desperate mind formed the plan quickly. She grasped at what she knew was her last hope. If only Suzanne had kept the original display plan, it just might work. There was no way to know if she'd make it, but Cassie knew she had to try. If she stayed where she was, it would only be a matter of minutes before she'd be found and killed.

Somehow, someway she had to be inside those windows when the lights came on.

The perfume bottle she hurled crashed, splattering loudly onto the floor behind the gun-wielding Santa. Cassie seized the precious moments she'd purchased, half running, half crawling past the remaining counters. She heard the music growing louder, and, despite the pain that racked her whole body, she rose and made one last desperate lunge toward the display windows.

Through the darkness, she stumbled up the steps and into the center of the window. The music was all around her. The cheers from the crowd rose like one huge helium-filled gasp. Strings of colored lights reflected off shining instruments as the musicians marched closer, closer.

Cassie heard a shuffling sound behind the darkened display. The band moved in front of the window. The twirlers tossed their batons high into the night air and in that instant the lights inside the window flashed on in one dazzling, sparkling, shimmering display of color and blessed light.

Cassie pounded frantically on the glass, shouting and screaming at the top of her lungs. The shrieking sound of raging madness behind her told Cassie her pursuer was upon her. She whirled around to see the Santa stepping up into the display, eyes blazing with rage. Cassie whispered a silent plea for deliverance as the murderer took final aim.

In the next frenzied instant, the sound of the explosion, the screams and shrieks of the crowd, and the shattering of glass rose to a deafening crescendo. Cassie felt a shower of glass raining all around her.

Paralyzed by the sight of the bizarre events taking place in front of her startled eyes, Cassie could only blink in dazed disbelief as she saw the gun fall to the floor and her would-be murderer collapse, crashing into the perfect line of wooden soldiers who tumbled in turn like dominoes out of the shattered window and onto the pavement.

Mind-numbing terror and confusion broke into blessed relief when she saw Mitch step up off the pavement and into the window. His gun was still in his hand as he bent cautiously over the inert form of the fallen Santa.

The crowd behind him gasped as he pulled the beard away to reveal the pallid face of Cassie's would-be murderer.

With a quick movement of his palm, Mitch closed the lids over Estelle Hahn's puzzled last expression. Cassie saw Lisa and Grant emerge from the crowd.

"I'm sorry," Lisa sobbed. "So sorry."

Grant Hahn stared down at his maiden aunt, his face as rigid and unreadable as one of his own department store mannequins.

"Don't move," Mitch ordered in a gentle whisper as he brushed away the tiny shards of glass that had fallen into Cassie's hair. When she finally released the breath she'd been holding, she felt for a moment as though the earth had slipped on its axis. But just as quickly, her world righted itself again when Mitch swept her up into his arms and stepped down onto the sidewalk.

When he lifted her left hand to get a better look at the ring she wore, his heart swelled and his eyes shimmered with emotion.

"I'm sorry I'm late," he whispered.

"Oh, Dempsey," Cassie cried, reveling in the embrace of the only man she knew she could ever truly love. "For once in your life, you're right on time!"

Epilogue

"Mmm, Dempsey, I do believe you've outdone yourself," Cassie purred as she sniffed the delightful aroma of the spicy western omelet crowded onto the plate he handed her.

"I aim to please, ma'am," Mitch drawled as he slipped back into bed beside her.

"Did I hear the phone earlier?" Cassie asked between bites.

"The hospital called. Ruth Palmer has finally come around. She's going to be all right. I spoke with Andy. He's already taken her statement."

"Oh, thank God," Cassie exclaimed, setting her fork down and reaching for his hand. "I can't tell you how I felt seeing her lying there, believing she was dead."

"You saved her life, Cass," Mitch said softly. "The blow Estelle delivered with the butt of that gun was deadly. If Ruth hadn't received help soon, she would have died."

"Why did Ruth call me, Mitch? Did she really have evidence to prove Jordan Sloane innocent?"

Mitch shook his head. "Sloane was the hit-and-run driver, I'll always believe that."

"He tried to kill me that night in the alley and again when he shot through my window and beheaded poor Samantha. He was my burglar, wasn't he? And the fire outside the aparment next to mine? Was he responsible for all of it?"

"He was your burglar, Cass. But it was a woman I saw on those stairs, I'm sure of it. Estelle must have started the fire. Thankfully she made the same mistake I did that first night I brought you home."

"Right!" Cassie exclaimed. "My name was still above the mailbox marked 304."

"Estelle masterminded everything. Her preoccupation with what she saw as her nephew's best interests was demented. He was the only family she had, the sole focus of her love."

"That isn't love. It's obsession," Cassie murmured. "So why *did* Ruth call me, Mitch?"

"According to what she told Andy, Ruth just happened to be in the wrong place at the wrong time. That night, she went up to the executive offices to print out another copy of the security report run the morning of the vandalism in the displays. As soon as she learned the truth, she was going straight to Grant."

"The truth? What did Ruth know?"

"At first, she wasn't exactly sure what she knew. But she'd seen Arthur changing the security printout that morning and she'd become suspicious. A few days later, she took the security system manuals home, determined to figure out how to run a copy of that report, herself. She'd just completed the printout and discovered it was Lisa who Arthur had been covering for when Estelle walked in on her."

"She was going to expose Lisa to Grant. She couldn't have known that he already knew," Cassie said. "Poor Ruth. She's really got it bad for that man."

"Anyway, Estelle had probably planned to call you herself, and bait you into coming up to the executive offices. Running into Ruth was a stroke of luck for her."

Cassie set her half-empty plate on the nightstand beside the bed and leaned back against the pillows. Mitch put his arm around her and drew her closer to him. Her skin felt like satin against his bare chest.

"Ruth made that call at gunpoint," he explained.

"No wonder she sounded so terrified." Cassie shuddered and he hugged her tighter. "Estelle had it all figured out," Cassie said. "The disgruntled intruder shot by the loyal secretary who gave her life for the firm."

"But Estelle made one fatal mistake."

"What's that?"

"She underestimated you," he explained, gazing into her eyes with an expression of open pride. "Estelle didn't realize that you'd do whatever you had to do, that you'd be willing take that final risk."

She stared into his eyes, and her deep love for him rippled through her in one long wave of desire. "But I'm through taking risks, Detective Dempsey," she informed him in a husky voice as she snuggled deeper into his embrace. "I've finally found a sure thing."

"You can bank on it, Mrs. Dempsey," he promised with a tender smile that pierced her heart with unspeakable joy.

He kissed her. The soft sunlight of that Christmas Eve morning filtered through the bedroom windows and cast their shadows against the wall. When he lifted his face, she touched his cheek and smiled.

And he kissed her again.

My Valentine
1994

Celebrate the most romantic day of the year with
MY VALENTINE 1994
a collection of original stories, written by
four of Harlequin's most popular authors...

MARGOT DALTON
MURIEL JENSEN
MARISA CARROLL
KAREN YOUNG

*Available in February, wherever
Harlequin Books are sold.*

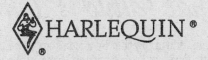

HARLEQUIN ®

®

VAL94

Valentine's Day was the best day of the year for
Dee's Candy and Gift Shop. Yet as the day drew closer,
Deanna Donovan became the target of
malicious, anonymous pranks.

A red heart was pinned to her front door with a dagger.

Dead roses adorned her car.

Soon, she was being stalked by her unseen admirer.

Suspicious of everyone, Deanna has nowhere to turn—and no
way to escape when she is kidnapped and held captive by her
Valentine lover....

#262

Cupid's Dagger

by Leona Karr
February 1994

You'll never again think of Valentine's Day without feeling a
thrill of delight...and a chill of dread!   CUPID

Curl Up With Someone Familiar

Familiar is back! The fantastic feline with a flair for solving crimes makes his third Harlequin Intrigue appearance in:

#256   THRICE FAMILIAR
by Caroline Burnes
December 1993

When a valuable racehorse is stolen from a horse farm in Scotland, it's Familiar's first chance to gain international acclaim. And it's the perfect opportunity for him to practice his pussyfooting panache, as he tries to matchmake the horse's owner and trainer, Catherine Shaw and Patrick Nelson—two people as opposite as cats and dogs!

Don't miss #256 THRICE FAMILIAR—for *cat*-astrophic intrigue and *purr*-fect romance!

FEAR-F